The Stolen Book

Sara Alexi is the author of the Greek Village Series.
She divides her time between England and a small village in Greece.

http://facebook.com/authorsaraalexi

Sara Alexi

THE STOLEN BOOK

oneiro

Published by Oneiro Press 2015

Copyright © Sara Alexi 2015

This edition 2015

This book is a work of fiction. Names, characters, businesses, organisations, places and events are either the product of the author's imagination or are used fictitiously. Any resemblance to actual persons, living or dead, events or locales is entirely coincidental

ISBN-13: 978-1517138530
ISBN-10: 1517138531

Also by Sara Alexi

The Illegal Gardener
Black Butterflies
The Explosive Nature of Friendship
The Gypsy's Dream
The Art of Becoming Homeless
In the Shade of the Monkey Puzzle Tree
A Handful of Pebbles
The Unquiet Mind
Watching the Wind Blow
The Reluctant Baker
The English Lesson
The Priest's Well
A Song Amongst the Orange Trees

Chapter 1

The slats of the unopened shutters offer Niki a narrow, panoramic view of the village. Whitewashed houses bask in the midday sun, red-tiled roofs shimmer in the heat, and a dry dust has settled over everything, diluting colours and bringing women out to their front patios and courtyards with brushes and brooms.

Up the road, in the top corner of the square, nestles the village shop, its door jammed open, inside too dark to see the well-used chair that waits for customers who want to linger and chat. Nor is it possible to make out the tumble of colourful clutter—the daily necessities stacked within, on which Niki and the rest of the village are so reliant. Propped in a plastic bucket by the entrance, shepherd's crooks catch on customers' shoulders as they enter, squinting. Just now, a stray dog, a white one with one light brown paw, lies in the shop doorway, the occasional customer stepping over him to enter.

But Niki's attention is on the *kafeneio* at the head of the square, which is gently buzzing, full of animated men. One by one, they take their leave, ready for their midday meal and afternoon sleep. From this distance, Niki recognises them by their gait, their heights, the greys and browns of their hair as they push and roll their shirt sleeves past the elbows or hitch up their baggy serge trousers. She cannot see Karolos, his dark hair usually so visible amongst his peers, and she continues her search as the men say their goodbyes to their neighbours, sitting in the same seats as yesterday, the week before, the year before that, their fathers before them. A nod or a lift of a finger reassures that they will see each other again.

If she leans her cheek against the shutter and looks to the right, she can see the tables and chairs outside the eatery next door. There is a dog there too, curled up at the base of the tree, which is wrapped around with fairy lights and which looks so pretty at night. It is too hot for any customers to sit outside today. Laughter comes from within and the radio quietly plays a *rebetika* accompaniment. These are the widowed farmers, the bachelors, and those needing a break from their wives. They have no dinners to return to so they go to Stella's eatery.

The smoky aroma of roast chicken from Stella's grill is rich and thick and makes Niki's stomach rumble. He'll be here soon, surely?

In the other direction, flanked with cottages that sink into the landscape, the narrow road leaving the village is straight as far as the primary school, where it curves sharply to the right past the multi-coloured railings. The corner is alive with boys bursting through the gates to run home as fast as they can and mamas chatting as their arms are pulled by small fingers eager for food and a *mesimeri* sleep. It is unlikely he would be in that direction. Their land is the other way, up towards the monastery.

A ribbon of sun filters back through the shutters, highlighting Niki's dark eyes. Her nose is in shadow but the delicate curve of her mouth is also illuminated as it twitches in and out of smiles in response to the village life being played out before her.

She pulls her head back as a butterfly crawls through the laths to find its way inside. The colourful creature circles the room in a dance, expressing joy at being alive, exploring the space until it is drawn back towards the light, fluttering too excitedly to find its way out again. After a moment it settles, exhausted, folding its red wings to reveal a mottled grey and black underside. If it were to crawl just one step, between the horizontal wooden bars, towards the sun, it would be free. But as the rays warm the tips of its feet, it explodes once again into life and its delicate wings make no impression on the unyielding shutters.

Niki reaches to save it, to open the shutters, to let it unleash its energy into the blue sky.

'Again!' Karolos flings himself onto the wooden kitchen chair, which creaks in response. Niki starts at his unexpected and sudden entrance and automatically picks up a tea towel, ready to take his lunch from the oven.

'Can you believe it? The ground was dry as a bone.' He struggles to unlace his boots. 'I should have gone out last night to check.'

Niki puts the *pastichio* on the table, a serving spoon beside it, and fills the glasses from a chilled jug from the fridge.

'Do you want to wait for the boys?' she asks. The issue with the watering system is not a new one. The *Dimos* turns the pressure down to stop the water being wasted at night when the tariffs are cheaper, but the result is there is not enough flow for the automatic systems to work and the farmers cannot water their trees in the cool of the night. The fruit dries and withers and it is not unknown for a farmer's yield to be halved, and with it his income.

'What am I supposed to do, go out with a bucket and water them one by one?' Karolos continues. 'Is this country that backward?'

Niki says nothing. They have been through this all before, and for now, he just needs to let off steam.

'If we had the money, we should build our own *sterna*, or drill, make a well,' Karolos grunts.

'Why don't you just water them by day? If we have no choice, what else can you do?' Niki takes forks from the drawer that does not close properly, the handle long gone, Karolos' baba's workmanship not standing the test of time.

'And how am I meant to know which nights there will be no water to know to water that day?' He rubs his hands vigorously up and down his face. The hair that was hanging loosely over his forehead perks up into a quiff as he runs his hands through his mane, pulling at the knots where it is longer at the back. He has always worn it long, influenced by the football players of the 1980s. 'The cost is double in the day, and the sun dries it up as soon as it wets the ground.'

Niki takes a deep breath and lets it out slowly. If she says anything, their frustration will escalate. He will shout, she will end up in tears, and they will argue. If only he just had a bit more force, a little more action. But he is content just to potter around the village all day long on his moped, accomplishing nothing, satisfied that the oranges will grow themselves, that the olive trees will produce as they have every other year, and then grumble about their problems, without ever actually doing anything about them.

Up until now, it is not the growing that has been the problem; rather, the selling. Actually, it has not been the selling—that is easy. The buyers come from Saros or beyond and agree a price and Karolos gathers together a gang of illegal immigrants to pick. The trucks are loaded and the oranges leave. It is getting paid that is the problem. Two years now, they have not received the money owed for the oranges. Karolos could have just been unlucky the first year, but to sell to the same man the following year?

'You know, sometimes I wonder how much you really value me and the boys.' Niki cannot hold herself back. 'You say you can do nothing, but there must be something you can do. I will take a bucket and do the watering myself if I have to.'

Karolos drinks down a glass of water and Niki refills it. The glass catches and reflects the sun that streams through the back door, which he has left open. The prisms of light flicker over his smooth skin. He is just as handsome as the day she met him, a bit more craggy perhaps, but with such a kind face.

A red chicken picks up its feet as it steps from their back yard of compacted mud into the shade of the kitchen. Karolos glances at it. Niki flaps a tea towel in warning, but it takes its time to retreat and as soon as her attention is elsewhere, the hen makes its way back inside, pecking at the floor by the side table where Niki cut the bread.

'You know, sometimes I wonder if you are not keen to send the boys to university in England. Are you not proud of them, that they have worked so hard, been offered places? You say it is no life to be an orange farmer and yet you do nothing to make sure that the boys will not follow in your footsteps. Do you want them to become orange farmers like you, not being paid for years, struggling to survive, a life of living hand to mouth?'

It is a bittersweet thought. If they study abroad, they will probably stay and work abroad, and it will give them a chance. The price of that chance is that she will miss them. Of course she will miss them. It will break her heart to have them so far away, but at least they will have a proper life, with choices, comforts.

'Of course I want them to go, but life is not so easy. We don't always get what we want.' Karolos' voice is gentle, always gentle, even when he is angry.

Niki can feel her limbs tensing. 'So what? We don't even try?'

'We are trying, Niki. What more can I do? I am taking the man to court to get paid, but you know that with the system as it is, it will take years and even then, what will make him actually pay the money even if the judge says he does owe us?'

'Why on earth did you trust him after he already owed us so much?' Her tears are flowing now, as they always do. The powerlessness she feels eats away at her until it squeezes out of her tear ducts.

'Niki, we are all trying to make a living, the man who bought our oranges just as much as us. So he had a bad year. We cannot judge him forever on that.'

'You are too good Karolos, too kind, too forgiving. You didn't have to sell to him again. You know what it makes me feel? It makes me feel you are more interested in pardoning him than you are in providing for your boys!' It has all been said before. The acid in her stomach burns and she sits down, exhausted with it all, putting her head in her hands.

'Niki my love,' Karolos leans across the table to touch her, stroke her hair. She looks up at him. He wipes away a tear with a gentle thumb. 'Niki, we will be alright. Always we will be alright. So we might have to adjust our dreams a little, but this is just life.'

The light in the room changes. Spiros stands in the doorway, Petros right behind him, their football shirts wet under their arms, boots in their hands.

Niki jumps up and takes plates down from the plate rack, all emotions on hold.

'Good day, boys?' Karolos asks.

'I'm starving. Can we eat?' Petros pushes past his brother to sit down and serve himself.

Chapter 2

She must hurry. Missing the first, and only, bus into Saros will mean taking a taxi, rendering the day pointless, as most of her wage will go on the fare. If Karolos could only carry a mobile phone, then at least she could call him, bring him out of the top orchards and get a lift on his moped. How many times has he left his phone in the hills under an olive tree or dropped it on stony ground?

The bus is just pulling to a standstill in the square as she hurries to meet it, as much as the first heat of the day will allow. School children jostle on in a lazy manner, subdued by the early hour. They talk quietly, some plugged into their own private worlds, nodding to the beats. Petros was one of these children last year. Now he no longer needs to take the journey with her. He has finished for the summer, his last exams taken, so when he is finally drawn from his bed, he will go with Spiros in friends' cars or on the back of a motorbike to enjoy the beaches and nightclubs; a daily ritual until September.

Cosmo grinds the gears of his moped to a standstill in front of the bus and, with a leg grounded on either side of his metal steed, his fingers walk through the letters in his leather bag. His post office badge hangs limply from his shirt, threatening to fall at any moment, his cap abandoned to allow his brow to sweat freely.

'Niki,' he says and holds out an envelope towards her. He stuffs the post bag back in the wire basket over the front wheel and drives off, only to stop across the road to deliver several letters to Vasso in the kiosk, next to the palm tree, in the centre of the square. Two illegal immigrants lounge on the circular wooden seat around the tree, arms over eyes as they snooze in its dappled shade. Having delivered the letters to Vasso, Cosmo abandons his bike and the post bag and ambles toward the *kafeneio* as if his day's work is done. Over the years, the post office has received a great number of complaints about late and lost mail.

Niki opens the letter when she is seated and the bus is moving away, the village quickly diminishing behind them. It is the heating bill for last winter, and she gasps at the amount. Another obstacle; the world conspiring against her. It seems every which way she turns, they owe money and every which way she looks, they in turn are owed money. How can they live, how can they make plans for the future if they never get paid for what they produce? Her jaw tightens, her teeth clench, and her tongue automatically finds the small, but slowly enlarging, hole at the back of one of her front teeth. Vasso in the kiosk, who seems to know a little about everything, suggested it could be from grinding her teeth at night. She has never caught herself doing this but most mornings she wakes with her teeth locked together so tightly, the muscles in her cheeks ache.

She consciously relaxes her jaw now, opening and closing her mouth without parting her lips.

The chatter on the bus grows in pitch as they pull to a halt to pick up more children from the next village. The bus judders as it moves off again and Niki watches the rows and rows of orange trees passing, the sun glancing off the shiny leaves, the ground under them pale and dusty, dry. The problem with the water affects all the farmers in the area.

The next trees are dark underneath and a hissing sound through the open window tells that a watering system is on. At this time of day, more than half of it will be lost in evaporation, nor will the tree take in all that it needs during the day and the oranges will not fatten. It is almost a waste of time in such heat—not to mention more expensive—but it is a desperate measure.

Last week, when the pressure was low three nights in a row, Niki ended up feeling particularly defeated, to the point where, on the third morning, she phoned the university in England to find out what would happen if the boys could not take the places they had won in September. It was a difficult conversation, as her English is reasonable but nowhere near fluent, but it was with relief that she understood that her boys could defer their places to the next academic year.

Well, if they don't get paid for last year's oranges soon and this year's fruits do not fatten, she will have to tell the boys that that is exactly what they will have to do.

These thoughts accompany her until the bus pulls up at the town's bus station.

Saros is always a bit of a shock to the senses. It is not a big town, but the pace is not quite as slow as in the village and the sun seems brighter and hotter as it glares off the pavements and the shop windows.

The mass of schoolchildren piles off the bus before her, the boys shouting and laughing now they have woken a little, calling each other names. The girls link arms, in no hurry, ambling, heads close together, engaged in intensely quiet conversations.

Taxi drivers fill the café chairs that spill onto the pavement outside the station, smoking endless cigarettes and drinking bottomless chilled coffees as they lean back to bask in the sun.

Too many drivers and not enough work.

Leaving behind the noise, Niki takes a back lane down toward the harbour. The cobbled road, hemmed in by stone buildings and bougainvillea-draped balconies, is too narrow for cars but the occasional motorbike leans on its own support, half blocking her way. She can see the sea peeking between buildings, sparkling, inviting. When summer is on its way, it never ceases to thrill her and today, the shimmering blue lifts her from her earthly concerns and fills her with a curious sense of optimism. A sense that there is something just beyond her grasp that will make her life totally different. A sense of impending change. There is no reason for this; nothing has altered. It is just a feeling, but her footfall lightens and she is in danger of skipping.

The grand buildings by the port, three and four stories high, have been converted into cafés and tavernas on the ground floor where they face the harbour, idyllic in the summer, buffeted by salted spray in the winter. Around the side or the back, these solid stone buildings boast tall, ornately carved wooden double doors which indicate the wealth of times gone by. The entire length of the port is fronted by these Venetian-influenced buildings, once homes for the rich. Now the money is made from the bars, and the rooms upstairs are mostly too noisy to be lived in and have fallen into disrepair. Some are used as storerooms for the tavernas below as the timber rots and the roof tiles slip.

As Niki approaches, she can see Kyria Toula on the balcony at the side of her mansion, one of only a handful that are still lived in. A boy on a moped has attached a basket of vegetables to a line hanging from the balcony above, and Toula is hauling it up with the aid of a small electric winch, which whines in complaint. There is an orange crate fastened to the back of the boy's moped with wire, and it is filled to overflowing with fluffy-topped celery, shiny, deep purple aubergines, courgettes carefully propped up to preserve their flowering ends, and other seasonal edibles.

'Thank you,' Toula calls down to the boy, who waits until the basket is over the balcony rail, and with a twist of his hand, revs his machine and putters away.

'*Kalimera*,' Niki calls up to her.

'Ah Niki. Here you are.' Toula fishes in her apron pocket and throws down a large key. 'That will save me coming down. That lift's still not working properly. Please don't use it, as it worries me.'

Picking the keys from the floor, as she has missed the catch, Niki heads towards the door. Inside, after the sun, it is shockingly dark and she must wait for her eyes to adjust. The relative cool makes her shiver. Just inside the front door, the ancient lift stands with its wooden doors wide and the metal concertina gates open. The floor is at an angle, and the whole thing looks unsafe. She would not go up or down in it even if Kyria Toula asked her.

With the light switch found, she begins her ascent up the wide staircase, the handrail smooth polished wood, the bannisters carved. She has never quite got over the grandness of it all and she always feels like an intruder as she makes her way up. The brass stair rods are still there, but a pale central section shows where a carpet would have once laid. She will sweep and mop down to the doors today; it is one of the jobs she only does once a week, which is illogical as it is the only place that really gets dirty with Kyria Toula and Kyrios Apostolis' comings and goings.

At the top of the steps, Niki composes herself before knocking. She smooths her hair, straightens her clothes, calms herself to a slower pace.

'Hello.' Toula opens the door with a smile. The light in the hall makes the old woman blink. Behind her is in semi-darkness, as all the shutters are closed, as always. The ticking of clocks fills the silence. The main room is large and it gets stifling hot with no air conditioning in the summer, and bitterly cold with the wind from the sea blowing through all the crevices and gaps in the winter. The room is panelled in dark wood, complementing the furniture.

If there was any light, the wood would shine with the amount of polishing it gets, but the shutters stay closed against the heat and the room is in perpetual gloom. They live in a half light. If it was not for the resonating ticking, a clock in every corner, time here would be standing still. Clocks are Kyrios Apostolis' passion. It is deafening when they all chime.

On one occasion when both Toula and Apostolis were out, Niki dared to open a shutter so she could actually see what she was doing. The wood of the antique furnishings was startlingly new looking in the sunlight, preserved, the sofas mummified. The glass faces of the clocks were shocked into mirroring the sunlight back and forth across the room, which suddenly came to life. The tapestries on the wall were vibrant with colour and the chairs Toula had covered herself years ago were very bright in design. If it was Niki's room, she would have the shutters open all the time.

Toula's head wobbles from side to side as she leads the way on unsure feet through the spacious room to the kitchen.

'Coffee?' she chirps and then quickly glances towards her husband. He is standing silently by one of the windows, one that has a shutter with a broken lath. He is using the single streak of light to read.

Not waiting for an answer from Niki, Toula is in her element, making coffee, rattling spoons, clinking china and generally adorning the kitchen table, which is strangely at odds with the rest of the house, with its yellow Formica top and chrome legs. The foods—a single soft, fluffy, dark red peach cut into slices; a small portion of feta dribbled with olive oil and a sprinkling of oregano; a couple of slices of fresh bread warm from the oven; a slice of cake with chocolate swirls running through it; a glass of freshly squeezed orange juice—are all displayed beautifully in order to tempt Niki. Toula herself won't eat, but she will drink a coffee and listen to news of the village where she used to live. Niki wonders why she ever moved. She is so keen to hear every detail of day-to-day life there.

The coffee is good. Toula deposits a cup by Apostolis, who grunts a thank you, still deeply engrossed in his book. After two years of working there, Niki has rarely spoken to him, or he to her. She prefers it when he goes out. His collection of clocks ticks around him, an external heartbeat, sometimes in sync, often not.

'Darling, I am just going out for a bit,' he suddenly announces and puts his book down on the nearest table.

'Will you be back for a snack, or shall I see you at lunch?' Toula enquires. But he does not answer her intelligibly. Then he is gone, the sound of the cogs and wheels of the ancient lift whirling and clanking, followed by the front door slamming shut. Toula visibly relaxes.

'Today, I have to go out, too. I am hunting for an English teacher.'

'Really?' Niki is genuinely surprised. Why would someone Toula's age want to learn a foreign language?

'I am hoping my granddaughter will come over this summer. It would be good to speak to her in English. My daughter lives there, you know? In London.'

'No, I didn't know,' Niki says and observes a part of her brain process whether this tenuous acquaintance could be helpful in getting the boys to university.

'And...' Toula says putting down her cup. 'Apostolis is having a clear out of his office. He has boxed up the books he is going to get rid of. I think he is going to give them to the school or Saros library or something. Anyway, he has made a real mess in the process. The shelves are filthy with dust, so if you wouldn't mind, just leave your usual routine and do his study today.'

Toula starts to clear the table.

'Leave it, Kyria Toula. I'll do it, and I'll pop away all these vegetables.' Niki picks up the basket that Toula hauled up from the street below on the balcony winch.

'You are a miracle,' Toula replies and, taking up her handbag, which is sitting on the counter, she scoops out a comb and with a few hard yanks through her white hair and the adjustment of some bobby pins, she waves a tiny goodbye and heads for the stairs.

Chapter 3

Upstairs, the top floor is no brighter. The shutters are kept closed here, too. The air is hot and musty and in the spindles of light that penetrate through chinks in the shutters, dust motes hover undisturbed. There is a vague smell of mothballs.

The hall floor is dark wood and uncarpeted like the rest of the floors, but behind the closed doors on this level, the bedrooms are insulated with rugs, warm for cold feet in the winter and to soundproof the main room below.

The first door on the left creaks open to reveal the guest room, which rarely needs any attention. With a flick of her duster, on Tuesdays, the surfaces are cleaned and the door is closed again until the following week. This is a Thursday, so Niki just checks to ensure there have been no surprise visitors that need tidying up after, or stray cups that have made their way in here, but as usual, all is neat. The door on the right opens into a large room: Toula and Apostolis' bedroom.

The sheets are pulled back over the end of the bed and there is an empty glass on one of the bedside cabinets. There is none of the usual bedroom jumble of clothes on a chair or coins and crumpled receipts on the dresser, as there is on Karolos' side of the bed at home. It takes just a pull and a twitch to make the bed and whilst she is there, Niki gives a sweep with her cloth to remove invisible dust from the bedside tables. Behind the door stands the carpet sweeper for the upstairs. Toula has told her that Apostolis thinks this old-fashioned implement is enough to keep the bedroom carpets clean if they are done every Thursday when Niki comes. It is an old cleaner, made of wood with double wheels down each side. It does little more than fluff up the pile of the rugs on either side of the bed, with most of the rotating bristles worn away.

Kyrios Apostolis' study is at the end of the corridor on the left. Niki has never been in here. The door is left ajar on occasion and she has looked in, but mostly Apostolis does not want his things touched.

In here, the air is stagnant and smells of suits that have been worn too long without being dry cleaned and books—old books. A click of the light switch makes the mess more apparent. Niki is about to start the clean up when, with a rebellious huff, she marches first to one and then the second window and throws both glass and shutters open wide. The sun streams in, hot but fresh, bringing all the smells of the ocean. A seagull wishes her a good morning in its flight as it passes the window on its way out toward the quilted water. A motorbike revs on the street below by the harbour. Waiters at the cafés call to each other, make small talk as they lay the tables with ashtrays and cocktail menus. In the bay, a small fishing boat labours and bobs, its putt intermittent, then a gurgling flat sound and silence.

There is that feeling again - the one of optimism, of hope beyond her wildest dreams. It flutters, playing in her stomach, gathers strength and begins to surge to her chest. Her fear that it has no reality drains some of its power but it remains strong enough to fill both her lungs, expand her chest. Her arms spontaneously reach for the beamed ceiling and with a big smile, Niki throws her head back and succumbs to the delicious feeling of hope or success. She is not quite sure which or what it is.

The boat's engine starts again and its puttering becomes part of the landscape. A horse-drawn carriage clops along the water's edge, with two large tourists sitting wedged in the back. Niki turns away from the sun-filled view to address the room. There are books everywhere.

Some of the shelves have been completely emptied. On the floor are boxes labelled *School*, *Library*, *Athens*, *Keep*. The desk is also piled with books and clocks, and balanced on top is a note Kyrios Apostolis has written to himself.

Sort books, give away those not wanted (School or
Library).
Clean shelves. Two behind the desk to display clocks.
Sort papers in desk.

The list goes on, referring to letters to be written, a bill to be paid. At least she has an idea of how to make the room look more presentable. There are clocks cluttering the spaces between piles of books, on the floor and the desk, mostly on the desk. If she can get the desktop clear, the room will feel much more organised. It is funny how after a few minutes in Toula's house, she no longer notices the ticking in every room. But she is always caught by surprise when they chime. If they were hers, she would co-ordinate them so at least they chimed at the same time, to shorten the ear-aching process.

There are a number of small clocks on a tray on the chair, presumably for display, too. The shelves are dirtier than they first appear to be, and the grime clings to her duster and she has to return to the kitchen, her shoes clacking nosily as she runs up and down the uncarpeted stair for more rags. She handles the clocks with great care and arranges them according to size, stepping back to admire her handiwork.

Perhaps she should take the boxes of books for the library and school downstairs, ready to go? But then this has not been specified, so maybe not.

Piling some of the books up carefully behind the door shows how dusty the central rug has become. Some of the boxes are very heavy. Grabbing the top of a cardboard box with *Library* written on the side, Niki lifts, bending her knees, trying to take the strain away from her back. It is heavier than it looks. Shuffling her feet, she moves across the room, arms extended down before her with the weight on her knees until she carefully lowers it on top of another box already against the wall. But as the books inside settle, the cardboard gives and splits down the corner, books spilling out over the floor. It was inevitable. Niki sighs.

A number of leaflets and pamphlets aid the cascade along, some with covers that have parted from their interiors. A hand-bound booklet covered with embossed interlocking knots intrigues her. She flicks it open and reads.

'Man's mind is like a garden. It can either be intelligently cultivated or allowed to run wild.' Niki blinks. It is handwritten, but it seems unlikely that it is Apostolis writing. Surely he wouldn't be sending something so personal to the library? She reads the line again. It has never occurred to her before that she has a choice of what runs through her mind. She reads on.

'Just as a gardener cultivates his soil, keeping it weed free and concentrating on the health of flowers and fruits for his own well-being, so must a man tend the garden of his mind, weeding out the harmful and useless thoughts, cultivating those he requires.'

'But why would anyone require specific thoughts?' Niki asks out loud. She flips over a page or two.

With raised eyebrows, she releases the front cover so it falls shut and stacks the booklet with the others behind the door. As she cleans, her head nods in agreement and understanding, digesting what she has just read.

With the room making progress, the feeling of hope and optimism returns. Now this is a thought, or rather a feeling, that she would like to control and encourage. Standing straight and easing her back, she looks out of the window, to the sky. But if she were to 'cultivate' her mind to think only these positive thoughts, it doesn't change the reality of circumstances, does it? She might feel good, but still the boys might not go to university in England. Is it enough just to be happy, feel hopeful, or does that hope have to bear fruit at some point?

She gathers up more books. The embossed booklet catches her eye again. Inside, the pages are worn, some torn, grease-embedded at the corner where pages have been turned, pages folded over and passages underlined with black pen.

The next page is titled *Getting Rich*.

'Getting rich,' she reads, 'is not solely a result of the environment that you live in or of the people you know. We know this because we see people rise from the most humble of beginnings to become rich and successful. Nor do we get rich from keeping our money close and not letting it go. No! Getting rich is all about the way you think.' This last sentence has been written in capitals and underlined several times. She takes the book to the desk and compares the writing with Kyrios Apostolis'. It is definitely not his writing. Apostolis' is angular, upright, whereas the writing in the book is swirling, curly, with big, round vowels.

'But I have found a way to become rich. It is a method, and I believe anyone else following what I have learnt will also grow rich. If they were to read my findings and follow my suggestions, by the time they have reached the end of all I have to say, their life will have changed.'

Niki swallows. What a thought! Life without the worry of whether they can afford to send the boys to university or not would be the one thing she would change right now. Everything else, she can put up with. She reads on.

'When I spend any time contemplating my desire for wealth, it occurs to me that life, all life, seeks more. Bacteria seek to multiply, rabbits increase in their warren, people want better jobs, bigger houses. Even those in the villages with such little expectation want the inside walls of their houses plastered to stop the mud mortar between the stones from cracking and falling. Everywhere I look, the natural desire is for more. And yet there seems to be an unspoken rule that says wanting more of riches is not natural. But it is, and how much more good people could do in the world where they had abundant wealth! I have found the only power they need to produce this wealth is their mind. The way they think affects the way they act, and that is the key.'

Niki sits in Apostolis' chair, immersed. The dust in the air settles. The sounds outside recede.

'Every thought we think creates our future. We have power to change that future even in this moment, in the very next thing we decide to do.'

'You up there?' Toula's voice rings up the stairs. Niki jumps up, eyes wide, looks around the room to reassure herself that she has made some progress. Toula's footsteps are on the stairs. Niki quickly scoops up the rest of the scattered books, clearing the rug, and then straightens the last of the clocks on the shelves. But, somehow, the book she was reading is back in her hand again. She wants to read more. Toula is on the landing, heading towards the study. If she puts the book back in the box, it might be in the library by next Tuesday. Or it might end up in a librarian's private collection, or the library might just put the whole box in storage. Whichever way she looks at it, the chance to read it might be gone.

'Ah, well, that was a waste of time,' Toula's voice calls from the corridor.

'I have power in this very moment, in the very next thing I decide to do,' Niki whispers to herself and then in an action that shocks her, she slips the book between the buttons of her blouse and wedges it in the waistband of her skirt.

'The woman's English was barely better than mine. I think she was Russian.' Toula leans on the door handle, half in and half out of the room, catching her breath. 'Oh my, doesn't this room look light with the shutters opened?'

'Oh I hope you don't mind. I can see better...'

'Oh course not, my dear. You must do what you need to do. Besides, it looks like you are making excellent progress. Carry on.' With this, she turns on her heel and potters back down the stairs.

It is only as Niki is finishing the cleaning of the study that her attention is drawn back to the book that is digging into her ribs, and she stops. Chewing on her lip, her hand slips inside her blouse to retrieve the book. She will replace it on the pile behind the door. But part of her, a part that is breathing heavily, turns her lip chewing into more of a snarl and she withdraws her hand, the book remaining hidden.

'You off now?' Toula asks as she descends the stairs.

'No, I was going to sweep and wash the main staircase.'

'Ah, Tuesday, dear. Do it next Tuesday.' Toula speaks as if she is tired and needs to be alone.

She overpays Niki, as usual. The Euros are fiddled out of a tight purse and pushed into her hand and then, despite Niki's protest, a few coins are added on top.

'For the boys,' Toula says and pats Niki's fist closed.

'Thank you, Toula.' Niki would like to return the book now. What kind of person would steal—and it is stealing, even if Apostolis no longer wants the book—from someone as kind as Toula? But there is no way to return it now without being obvious. She will bring it on Tuesday and hope the boxes of books are still there.

'Oh, Kyria Toula,' Niki shouts back up the stairs when she is almost on the street. 'You could try the English lady Juliet in the village, for your English lessons. Shall I tell her to call you?'

Toula expresses what a kind and good girl she is and, hidden in the dark of the stairwell, Niki's cheeks grow hot. She does not wait until Toula has finished praising her before she closes the door and heads for the bus station with the book digging heavily into her ribs.

Chapter 4

Usually she would go straight home. Where else would she go? Sometimes she goes to the corner shop and ends up chatting with Marina or Marina's daughter-in-law Irini, enjoying the relief offered by the air conditioning in the shop. Sometimes she goes over and talks to Vasso in the kiosk, and most Tuesdays and Thursdays, she spends some time sitting outside the eatery next door to her house with Stella or dear old Mitsos as they serve the farmers inside and tend to the grill. But that is not actually going anywhere; these are just stops on the route home.

What's more, she needs to start cooking. Karolos will be home in an hour or two, hungry, and the boys will finally heave themselves out of bed, fuzzy haired, in nothing but their tracksuit bottoms, complaining that they are starving because they didn't eat the night before when they were out with their friends. This morning, they did not come home until six o'clock, when the air was already becoming hot and still.

It is understandable at this time of year that they live at night. It is just too hot to do anything during the days. There is a whole group of them that meet up in the late afternoon, usually for a swim down at Saros town beach. The boys diving and splashing, the girls lounging and tanning. Later, they go on to one of the souvlaki grill shops and, for a couple of Euros, eat pita bread wrapped around tomatoes, chips, onions, *tzatziki*, and grilled meat that has been sliced off the stack that sizzles, slowly rotating in front of the electric grill. Then they hang out at bars and later still at the *bouzouki* clubs out of town along the coast road in the cool night air. Niki would have loved to have done the same thing at their age.

Come daylight, there are no buses to get them home and most mornings, the phone rings at four or five and Karolos rolls out of bed to rattle off for them in the farm truck, bringing the boys back in the cab with him and their friends often on the back. Karolos never complains. It is better than relying on the motorbikes or cars of friends who might have been drinking.

God, how she would have loved to have had such indulgence at that age. Athens, for her, was far from friendly. In truth, the time she wishes to forget was only a short period: two months, maybe three, but it was enough to change her. The days, thankfully, have blurred and the images faded as the years have passed and she has long ago forgiven her parents for not having given her the option to stay in her small hometown village just north west of Permeti. They argued that with the 1992 election and the end of Communist rule, she must take advantage of the new freedom to travel and leave the war-torn area.

'Go Niki. *Zemra ime*. Go take from life what we could not,' her *Očka* had said, and then he went on to say that there were jobs to be had abroad and what she could earn would not only help them in their old age but really set her up for a good future in Albania if she were to return. Maybe she would only have to be away a year, or two at most, then she could send back enough for them to build a house for her. But their words of hope and optimism did not ring true. Their heads were filled with experiences and memories of the olden days and she was sure some part of them believed that by leaving the country, it would be assured that nothing tragic would ever happen to her. Their fatigue showed in their faces, in the slowness of every movement. Life had beaten them, but somewhere in their damaged, twisted logic, they felt that if she left, she would be free and in that freedom, they would be free, too.

At the time, she had no intention of going. The village was her home; her parents and childhood friends who surrounded her were her world. Why would she leave now that there was a new government, a new start? She was young and full of life and energy and hope.

Despite her loudly voiced objections, *Mumija* and *Očka* did not let the subject drop. At one point, sitting on the porch, listening to the sounds of the small village as they shelled peas, *Mumija* had described how her elder sister had been taken to the rape camps operated by the Bosnian Serbs. Her voice was so small as she spoke, Niki leaned in to hear, the emotion squeezing her *Mumija's* throat, almost silencing her.

At some point, Niki stopped shelling the peas and stared instead at the range of mountains fading into the distance, each half covered with scrubland and stunted bushes, bare earth where the spring rain had washed away whole sections. With summer not yet upon them, the rivers still flowed deep at the valley bottoms, brown with earth that would be deposited in the fertile plains nearer the sea. The countryside was ever changing as the hills around them slowly eroded.

Mumija's voice came back in focus.

'When they finally let her go, the foetus was grown too large to be aborted. She shot herself in the head two weeks later.' Niki returned her attention to the peas, not knowing what to say as *Mumija's* tears splashed over her fingers as she worked. When the peas were finished, she dried her face on her apron and spoke again. Niki was afraid of being told more; she did not want to hear these ugly tales of the past, and the anger growled inside her for being made to listen.

'Niki, my love, we have a sort of peace now but for how long? This country, Yugoslavia...'

'It's not Yugoslavia now. We are not at war, *Mumija*,' Niki began, the anger trying to escape.

'For how long? We have been at war forever,' *Očka* murmured and stood behind *Mumija* at this point, a hand on her shoulder, his eyes watching the back of his wife's head. *Mumija's* eyes scanned the floor as the memories tore through her mind.

'But now we are not at war.' Niki tried to deflect her, alter the direction of the conversation.

'You have no idea what it was like. The Serb forces had the support of their commanders. They were ordered to rape.' *Mumija* gasped. *Očka's* grip on her shoulder tightened, but it did not stop more tears that came with her words. 'It was a tactic to make sure the people would not return to the area. They would bear a child of the enemy. Victims were told they would be hunted down and killed should they report what happened. My sister, your aunt...' But she could not continue and she buried her face into *Očka's* stomach, who stood by her, solid, unmoving, his beard glistening with his own tears.

'There is a group going to Greece,' he said as *Mumija* continued to silently cry, her face hidden. 'It would be a chance to work, save a little money, and in a year or two, when we are sure of the peace, you can return. Until then, it would help if you would send a little something to us. We are getting old to work such long hours. What will become of us when we are too old to toil?'

Purposely missing the point—and with the sureness of youth—she protested that the days of war were over, that they must not look back.

'To be angry is to be a victim,' she told them. 'Do not let yourself be violated by the memory like you were violated by the act.'

How insensitive, how young and arrogant she must have seemed to tell them how to deal with their sorrows, the horrors they had seen. She had no idea of what they had been through. How could she? Nor did she ever expect to experience anything like they had. But then, as life would have it, she had gone with that group to Greece and suffered her own abuse.

With a glance in the direction of the house, she turns off the village square and heads up the hill. The road here is lined by whitewashed walls, the lime paint applied year after year until it is on so thick, it coats the stones like icing on a cake and makes the base look at if it is melting into the soil.

Halfway up the hill on the right is Mitsos and Stella's place. The brass handle atop the letter box made from an old drawer glints in the sun and a lizard half covers it, basking in the heat. Its tongue tastes the air but it does not scuttle away as she passes. Past the post box on the gate and down the rutted drive, Stella and Mitsos' cottage nestles among the almond trees beyond. Geraniums grow in painted pots all around the compacted mud back yard. To the front of the cottage, overlooking the village, a table and chairs fade in the sun. Stella has been a good friend over the years, but Niki is very happy that her first husband Stavros is gone and that she has married the kindly old Mitsos.

Past the gate, the track continues up to the top of the hill, where it peters to nothing amongst the pine trees that tuft the brow like hair.

The view from here fills her heart and the feelings of hope and change intensify. The village, like a toy town, is mapped out at her feet, the many layers and levels of red-tiled roofs dominating the whitewashed walls from this bird's-eye view. Beyond the village, the orange and olive groves checker the plain and, far away, the mountains fade purple and hazy into the sky. To her left, the bay scoops a blue bite out of the landscape and Saros town sits at the point where the calm waters open out into the sea. Saros town, providing both lookout and guard, Niki likes to think, keeps their village safe.

The ground under the trees is deep with pine needles, like a cushion to sit on, releasing their rich fragrance in the warmth of the sun. With her legs out in front of her and her hands behind, she lets the sun heat her face. Her fingers dig into the soft ground covering and she remains motionless until an insect crawls over her fingers, making her jump. It is enough to bring her back to the present. Feeling between the buttons of her blouse, she finds the book, takes it out, and opens it.

Chapter 5

'The past cannot be changed,' the books says. 'The future is shaped by our current thinking. The way we think is based on how we see ourselves. How do you see yourself?'

Niki looks up from the book, out at the plain that is touched by the sea, at the village that she now calls home.

'How do I see myself?' She addresses all that is in front of her. 'As a mama who is not providing for her children.' She sighs and returns to the book.

'What beliefs about yourself did your parents give you?' the black and white ink demands.

She shuts the book. She will return it tomorrow.

All her parents gave her was a sense that life should be feared. They filled her head with the notion that the world was not a safe place. So busy were they keeping her safe that they never stopped to listen to how she saw the world or to notice how the world had changed. They took her voice away, stifled who she was, denied her opinions—all in the name of 'keeping her safe' and then, in the ultimate act of trying to keep her from harm, they pushed her out into a world she was not ready for, to travel with strangers to an unknown country where their expectation of her was not only to find a job but to earn enough to send a little back to them.

'Where were those jobs?' Her voice is a whisper as she blinks away a tear. 'And they just sat back at home, sitting there waiting for money.'

A man leads a donkey through the village streets below her. The donkey changes colour from grey to black as they pass under the shade of the palm tree in the square.

The small bus she was helped onto in Albania had taken a group of ten of them. *Mumija* packed her suitcase, more full of food than clothes. *Mumija* cried and *Očka* waved and continued to wave even when she could see his arm growing tired. But sitting with her nose pressed against the bus window, she had refused to acknowledge them. Her sadness at leaving, her fear of being alone, and her anger at being manipulated had frozen her to a place where she could no longer respond. The sense of abandonment started before her suitcase was even packed. The empty hollow of her desertion at first shocked her and then unravelled her, draining her power, her belief, even, at times, her reason to keep breathing.

The bus that juddered out of the square, making her parents' faces grow smaller and smaller, turning their bodies into nothing but black dots, was an old one and after only an hour, they had to keep stopping to let the engine cool down. The whole journey was meant to take eight hours with an hour's break in Lamia. But by the time they reached Athens, it had been over fifteen hours stuck in that bus, by which time the run-down hostel they were heading for was locked up for the night and slowly everyone melted into the shadows, leaving her alone to wait for dawn by the brightly lit entrance to the metro station.

Four days later, her money was gone and there was no job. Every place with a job to offer had a dozen Albanians to choose from.

'Go to the islands,' someone said.

'In the southern Peloponnese,' another suggested.

'Anywhere but Athens,' they all agreed, but she had no way of getting anywhere without money now.

Niki opens the book again.

'It is important to note that your parents did the best they could with what life had offered them and with the knowledge they had. They had their own childhood, which made them the way they are, and you had yours that made you who you are. The cycle of blame can therefore be endless unless you decide it must stop. Laying the blame for your life at their door is to continue to be a victim. To blame any part of your life on your past is to be a victim because right now, you have the power to be whoever you want to be. Now is the moment.'

But isn't that what she did back then when she landed in Athens? Take what power she had at the time, and where had that got her? With no job and no way to get to a job, the offer of a bed for the night was better than sleeping in a doorway. She knew what the price was when he offered. It did not seem offensive; it was all part of the same nightmare. She became subject to an alternate reality and, she can remember the surreal feeling even now, nothing that happened to her mattered because by then, she did not matter.

If she had mattered at all, her parents would never have made her take the journey.

In retrospect, she was lucky that he was not a bad man, just lonely and, if she was honest, he did not take such an advantage of the situation. He cuddled her as they spooned together in his dark, one-roomed apartment. He wriggled a bit, tensed, shuddered and relaxed, and with a loud exhale of breath fell into a deep sleep. That was that, or so she thought. But when she woke in the morning, as he hurried her out the door, he handed her a fist full of Euros and said if she was around that night, after he got back from work, perhaps she would like to stay again.

If she had been asked at the time what she did for a living, she would never have seen the truth. It was only later, when, by this method, she raised enough money to travel to the Peloponnese, found herself a job in the souvlaki shop, and met Karolos that an ugly word for what she had been doing popped into her head.

The word, even now, all these years later, with two grown boys, makes her lose focus and sets her insides trembling. It tightens the muscles across her chest and hastens her limbs to become busy, do something, anything other than think those thoughts. If it had only been this one man, it would not have been so bad, but as what she was doing, which she told herself was just a cuddle and sleep, began to seem almost normal in this alternate reality in which his friend had been introduced. The friend wanted to sleep curled up with her too, he had said. But that was not all he truly wanted. He was more demanding and she felt she was in no position to make her own demands. And in this way, her innocence was ground into grubby, seed-stained sheets.

At that time, all her energies were concentrating on existing, but, after a while, she even lost her enthusiasm for that. The direction her life was going was apparent and even in those few short weeks, what she was doing did enough damage for her to no longer care.

The book sits in her lap. She should go home really, start cooking. These thoughts are depressing. Her thumb is still against the next line, so she reads on.

'Whatever we believe comes true for us. If we believe we can, then we will. If we believe we can't, that is also true. If you have no love, it is because you believe you do not deserve love, and if you have no money, it is because you believe you do not deserve money.'

That hurts.

Not the love bit. She knows she is loved by Karolos and by the boys. But the part about money seems to chime within her.

Stuffing the book back in her waistband, she heads back down the hill. Thinking about what to cook for her family blocks everything out. She will have to make something that does not take long to cook. Spaghetti Putanesca, that's quick. She snorts a sad laugh. *Putana*. That's the word that makes her lose focus. A quick wipe banishes the tear before it makes it too far down her cheek and by the time she is at the square, she is wondering if she has enough spaghetti for her three boys.

It is as she is gathering a handful of basil from the pots of herbs she grows around her back door that she realises that what resonated within her with regards earning enough money was that she does not feel she deserves, or rather wants money because it is, in her experience, dirty. Money equals squalid humiliation.

'Oh what!' she exclaims out loud to herself in her realisation. It is as if those dark days have come back to punish her. Neither the boys, nor Karolos, know anything about that brief time, nor ever will they. But right now, it feels that this must be life's way of getting even, making her pay, or rather making her boys pay, for her past sins.

'No!' She pushes the back door open, takes a pan down from where it hangs on the wall, and slams it on the cooker top.

'No!' she repeats, addressing the world. 'No you don't. They are going to England.' With which, the chopping board is slammed with equal passion and noise on the scrubbed table top.

The boys are up before Karolos is back and they droop around the kitchen in their jogging bottoms, all muscular and tanned and beautiful and her anger changes into determination, strengthened with the love she feels for her children. 'No way,' she hisses under her breath.

Chapter 6

After their late lunch, the boys persuade Karolos, despite his sleepiness, to give them a lift into Saros town, and Niki contents herself with doing the washing up, finding the cool of the water refreshing. She watches the chickens scratching at the crumbs she threw out into the back yard. One day, one far and distant day, they will concrete the back yard, or pave it, have ceramic plant pots instead of painted olive oil tins for the geraniums.

She has not finished in the sink for long when Karolos returns, dropping the truck keys on top on the first pile of pots she washed that quickly dried in the heat, all ready to put away, and declares he is going for a sleep. Their bedroom door closes softly behind him. She can hear him kicking off his boots, two thuds as they hit the bare wooden floor. The springs of their bed creak as his weight depresses them, the walls are so flimsy. The three-roomed house has been too small for them since the boys first found their own feet and it cannot be easy for her sons to share a room at this age. They need their privacy. How many hours have she and Karolos spent planning what they would do if they ever had any money? It used to be their regular Saturday night entertainment. With a bottle of wine between them, they would fantasise, dream dreams, even make little drawings. They would erect a second floor, they said, one big open space with wooden roof beams the colour of honey. This will be the sitting room and kitchen combined. If it takes up the whole footprint of the house, it will be huge, and they could build out over the donkey shed to have a spacious balcony with a view across the village towards the sea. Downstairs, they would divide the kitchen and living room with a wall so they would have three bedrooms and an area for the boys to relax in, use the computer, play video games. The external stairs up to the roof could be made enclosed to access the second floor, the original front door moving outwards towards the garden gate. Then they would dream up the details: an open fireplace for winter, a huge air-conditioning unit for summer, and they would go to bed happy, believing that one day, somehow, it was going to happen.

She doesn't believe the dreams any more.

It's not as if the present sitting area is even big enough for them all. They have the day bed and one chair, so if they watch a film together, one lies, one sits and the other two must content themselves in the kitchen area on wooden chairs around the table. Is this really what her parents imagined for her when they insisted that she leave Albania?

With the dishes put away, she falls into a stare, looking at a geranium cutting that is finding its roots in a cut-down water bottle for a pot on her windowsill in front of the sink. It probably needs watering. She will do that this evening when it is cool. She pulls herself back into the present and remembers the book which she put on the shelf with her well-used Greek cookbook. She is not sure if she is amused or horrified when it occurs to her that that is also a stolen book. She can still remember searching the library shelves for it, nearly twenty years back now.

When they were first married, Karolos, very gently and very sweetly, with kisses and hand holding, told her that her cooking was not like the dishes his mama used to make. For a while, she did not know what to do; she only knew how to cook what *Mumija* had taught her—Albanian dishes. She felt a bit embarrassed to ask her neighbours so in the end, by pure chance when trying to find the office where she must pay the water bill, she discovered the tiny library in Saros town.

The library shelves were sparsely populated and naturally, the majority of the books were in Greek, which at the time she could speak but only read with great effort. Her written Greek improved later, when her boys began school and she sat daily with them, struggling over their homework. She learnt as much as they did, as she was always trying to stay one step ahead.

So when she was in the library searching the shelves for a cookery book, she was hoping to find one with step-by-step pictures, but as luck would have it, she found one written in English, something she excelled at back in school. She was delighted and used it daily, learning and improving both her culinary and her language skills. Karolos, bless him, was so complimentary, he made it a joy for her to try.

But somehow, the book, after being used several times and every page learnt almost by heart, never made it back to the library, and no one asked her for it.

Leaving the ragged cook book where it is, she takes down the thinner book, the one from Toula's.

'Come on then, you said you would change everything if I followed what you said, so let's see what I must do.' She speaks to the unknown and unseen author. Pulling out a kitchen chair, she shades her eyes from the sun streaming through the window and studies.

Decide to change is the title of the first section.

'What you do is directed by what you think. You need the skill to think what you want to think rather than let thoughts flit through your brain. Taking this control takes effort. But when you think of wealth and riches, do not want them for their own sake or to live a hedonistic lifestyle or to outdo others because if this is what you are striving for, then the world will not help you. Your desire for wealth must be for the simple reason that you want to better yourself and better the lives of those around you.'

'Well, I want to be a better mama, and I want more for my boys. They have done their part, working hard, getting the grades and being offered places. Now I must do mine. Provide a way for them to go. There cannot be a purer motive than that!' Niki tells the book.

Karolos snores gently and a donkey brays its lonely call somewhere out in the village. Its strangled cries go on for far longer than it sounds as if it has the breath for, stopping as suddenly as it started.

'Come on, how about some practical help, and less of this mystical stuff,' she says to the book.

'If you want something, speak of it as if it is already yours. Claim it before it arrives. Link this to becoming all you can be for mankind and as a whole person, and then your every action will be towards this goal.'

'Very helpful,' Niki huffs and stuffs the book back on the shelf and, pulling off her apron, goes to lay down on the day bed. Karolos' snores are muffled behind the door and then with a ping of springs, he turns and all is silent.

The shutters are closed to keep out as much afternoon heat as possible, but the sun streaks horizontally through the gap at the bottom, its rays slicing the floor into pieces. She lies on her back. There is a plume of cobwebs in one corner, and someone has knocked the framed photograph of her boys, aged about ten, at an angle on the wall by the old television on top of which she notices someone has left a glass of water. But for now, everything must stay as it is as her eyes are closing.

The back door is open when she wakes and one or two of the chickens are cleaning the floor around the stove. There is a note on the table.

'Beautiful even when you sleep.'

It is Karolos' writing. He is such a sweet man. Sweet and kind, but why can he not just get a bit more excited about life? Has he rung the Tasso who owes them for the oranges today? Haven't they talked about this?

'People do what they feel most hassled to do,' Niki argued.
'It's just not nice though, to call a man every single day.'
'It's not nice to take the oranges and then not pay.'
'Ah, but his mama has been sick.'
'And we have boys that need educating.'
'The boys are fine.'
'The boys need to go to England.'
'If they want to go, they will go.'
'They won't be able to go if we have not got the money.'
'Niki, you worry too much. It will all be fine, you will see.' And with this, he left the house and did not come back until after the sun had set.
'Gorgeous but useless.' Niki rubs her face to full wakefulness.

She could set about doing the ironing. There is always a never-ending pile with the two boys. They often change their shirts twice a day in this heat, and the washing machine goes on at least once a day. What would she do without it? Now it has developed a rattle that was not there last month. It is just a matter of time.

The heat of the day has subsided and Niki cannot face standing still for an hour or two with the shirts. Instead, she will go to Juliet's and tell her that Toula is looking for an English teacher. It is always nice at Juliet's. Her house has such a calm and airy feel.

She waves to Vasso as she turns right after the kiosk and does not go far before she takes a left along the old dried river bed. This widens out into a small square, a house on either side and in the top right hand corner, so narrow you almost miss it, is the track up to Juliet's.

The track passes four houses on the left and is flanked by a continuous wall on the right—the backs of cottages that have their own track at the front. The first house on the left has been empty for some time, the grass grown as tall as she is and dried brown in the heat, the palm tree's bottom leaves hanging to the ground, also brown and peeling off the trunk, and the path up to the door is littered with bits of paper and leaves. The next house has a garden and courtyard bursting with flowers, bright pinks next to poppy reds alongside bougainvillea in orange and white, the riot of colours so happy in the sunlight. Kyria Georgia, who lives here, tends her blooms to perfection. The next cottage is only occupied in the summer. The owners have a bookshop in Athens and come down more and more rarely as they grow older. The final house before Juliet's is an old barn that has been converted into a holiday-let cottage with a roof that slopes down almost to ground level by the track. Behind the house glimmers the blue of a pool. Niki cannot imagine what it must be like to be so privileged.

A metal arch over the gate announces Juliet's old stone cottage at the end of the lane. Wild roses grow over the arch from one side and from the other, more bougainvillea. The gravel drive leads up to the shaded patio. Juliet, sunglasses on, is stretched out on an old sofa that she drags outside for the summer. A cat sits on her lap and her head is resting back on the arm. There is a chance that she might be asleep. Perhaps she should have phoned first.

'Oh, hi. Oh, dear, I think I must have nodded off.' Juliet lifts her head and takes her sunglasses off to rub her eyes. The cat lifts its head and then goes back to sleep.

'Shall I come...'

'No, no, come sit. What can I get you? Water, frappe?'

'No, nothing. Thanks,' Niki says, the flat of her hand suggesting that Juliet should remain sitting. 'I just came to tell you of someone who wants English lessons.'

Chapter 7

'Is it Tuesday already?' Karolos asks as Niki gets ready to go to Toula's house. She is late again and will miss the bus unless she hurries.

'I haven't fed the chickens yet.' Niki grabs the book from the shelf and puts it in her bag.

'I'll do it.' His arms reach out to hold her, to kiss her before she leaves, but if she does not go right now, the bus will leave without her.

'Sorry,' she mutters, breaking free and running out of the house. She has to wave down the bus as it is just moving away, the children having taken the majority of the seats so she sits directly behind the driver, her bag on her knee, the book peeking out. Slipping onto her knee, it opens to the page she last read.

'Your desire for wealth must be for the simple reason that you want to better yourself or the lives of those around you.'

No, she has read that bit. Move on. The orange trees flash past the windows of the bus, dark underneath. The water pressure has been strong enough over the last few days to water. They need it to continue.

'You do not have to take anything away from anyone else to grow wealthy. There is no need to treat people unfairly. Always give more than you receive, but not in monetary terms. Give in a way that the receiver will consider what they received to be greater than the value they are paying. If your mind is focused on this, then opportunities will come your way.'

Closing the book, Niki tries to work out what that is meant to mean. She already gives Toula more than she ever asks, doing extra jobs, helping with the grocery deliveries and the dry cleaning to the point that Toula always pays her extra. There is nothing more she can do unless she asks Toula for more hours or for a pay increase. Maybe that is what she should do, even though she is getting a fair wage already. A woman gets on with a sack that is almost as big as she is, which she slides, kicking it with her feet until she can sit down and brace it between her knees.

'Do not try to apply power to things outside of yourself. It is wrong to do so. You must only apply pressure on yourself.' The book is getting more and more mystical. Maybe this is why Kyrios Apostolis is getting rid of it. He is bound to have read it and his final conclusion is to give it away. He is probably right. Well, she is returning it, so that will be that.

The bus pulls into Saros bus station. The taxi drivers fill the street-side café as usual. There is a group of back-packers waiting for the bus to Athens, talking quickly to each other, excited, nervous. The blond hair and long legs in shorts distinguishes them from the Greeks who, shorter and darker, move languidly. Niki pushes her way through the throng and onto the back street that leads down to the harbour side.

As she approaches the house, Toula is standing by her door.

'Well hello, and thank you so much. Juliet and I have talked and I am going for my first lesson.' She seems excited and holds the door open for Niki to go in. 'The Apostolis is out and I will be back in the hour,' she says in English, each word pronounced slowly but clearly. 'You have the breakfast on the table and the coffee is new. Please to sit before you do the work.'

Niki laughs and Toula joins in.

'Was it that bad?' Toula asks.

'No, it is wonderful that you are learning.'

Toula's head wobbles from side to side. Niki wonders if the spontaneous movement annoys her. Perhaps she is not aware of it. Toula pats her on the shoulder and hobbles off.

Laid out in the kitchen is a breakfast fit for a king. Toula is good to her word and as Niki sits to eat, she takes the book from her bag to remind herself to return it. She opens it at a random page as she eats.

'Do not talk of others as being poor. Only as people who are becoming richer, this will create a positive feeling around you and you will draw the people you need towards you. You can make the world a richer place by being rich yourself and with this attitude, you will draw other rich people into your life who will help your progress. But as you speak of others as if they are becoming rich, do not be in competition. Your riches will come by being creative and by doing so, you will show others how they too can find creative ways to grow rich.'

The clocks tick as she digests this paragraph.

'Almost,' she tells the clocks and the polished wooden furniture. 'It almost makes sense.' She can imagine that if she talks of her fellow man as if all good things are coming their way, she will create a very positive atmosphere around her. It may well result in people seeking out her company. She nods in agreement. 'Yes, it could easily follow that opportunities could come my way as a result.' Her brow furrows as she contemplates. She tidies the table, deep in thought, her mind dwelling on what she has just read. She washes up her pots and readies her cleaning things, mulling over the possibilities. Book in hand, she goes to the study, where it needs to be returned to.

The room is immaculate. The clocks tick more quietly here, the shelves are ordered and dusted, the rug swept, and everything is in its place. There are no piles of books to be got rid of, no boxes to be taken to the library or the school. Everything is in order. There is nowhere to put the book. Maybe she could just return it to one of the shelves. But on inspection, it appears that the books on each shelf are arranged in alphabetical order, each row with a different topic. There seems to be no obvious place for the book so she slips it into her waistband until she can decide what best to do.

She polishes woodwork that needs no polishing, wipes away dust that isn't there, changes sheets that do not need changing. The only satisfaction she gets is in chasing the dirt on the stairs down to the front door. When she opens the door to brush the dust out, a cat tries to gain entry.

'Oh no you don't, my friend.' She gently stops it with the end of her broom. Toula is coming towards her up the cobbled street, and she smiles when she sees the cat.

'Oh, that naughty animal,' she says when she gets closer. It makes a dash to get inside and Niki grabs for it. As she does so, the book falls from her waistband and in a flash, her cheeks grow red.

'Oh my dear, you have dropped your book.' Toula slowly bends to pick it up. Niki hesitates and watches the old woman slowly bend to the ground to retrieve it, straightening up even more slowly. Niki desperately tries to think of any reasonable excuse that would not amount to admitting that she is a thief. Even to say she borrowed it without permission is not good.

Toula looks at the book and then at Niki and opens her mouth to speak but just as she does so, up the stairs, behind them, the clocks begin to chime. First the big grandfather clock in the sitting room, then the mantelpiece clock joins in, and then, one by one from all over the house, others accompany and Toula stops speaking and waits. Niki's stomach turns over. Still no excuse will come to mind. The best thing is just to be honest, say it caught her eye, she took a look, forgot to put it back, which is not totally untrue, and that she has it with her now in order to return it. Yes, she must be honest. Even the book said that: *Do not take from someone else to grow rich yourself*, or something along these lines. *Be creative*, it said. With a few whirrs and clicks, the clocks come to the end of their drawn-out symphony and the chimes fade. If she has an excuse, better to say it now before Toula speaks. But she is too slow.

'Your book, my dear,' Toula says. 'It is so nice that it is possible to read books these days. When I was a girl... no, not even then. Only a short while ago in the nineties, books were so expensive that it was cheaper to photocopy them than to buy them. There were little shops in the back streets here in Saros and many in Athens where that was all they did, a man and a photo copier, and they would stand all day turning over the pages of a book to copy each page. Half a day's work a book and still it was cheaper than buying them.' She passes the book to Niki, whose hand shakes as she takes it.

'Thank you,' is all Niki can mutter.

'Oh, and thank you for suggesting Juliet. Such a nice lady. By the way, I bumped into a friend of mine yesterday who works at the water board. Now, I do not know your position but to offer you a little something in return for your kindness in suggesting Juliet, I want to tell you that my friend did tell me that she was giving in her notice at the end of the week. It is only a part-time job, so hopefully you will also stay on working here, but I did wonder if you wanted another little job?' Toula's eyes shine. 'Oh, look how lovely the stairs are when they are clean. I hope you avoided the lift? Are you all done?' As usual, it is not a question. She moves slowly, tired from life, not just from exertion. The cat runs past them both and up the stairs.

'Yes.' Niki follows Toula's slow tread up the stairs, puts the book down on the kitchen table, takes her apron off and hangs it up, washes her hands, and picks up her bag. Toula hands the book to her for a second time and with it, her pay.

'A little something extra for putting me in touch with Juliet. Thank you so much.'

Niki wants to contest the offer but Toula shakes her head and sits down.

'I will see you next time,' she says, but she is looking at the floor as she speaks. The English lesson must have taken all her energy. Niki wishes her '*Kalo mesimeri*' and leaves.

Once in the street, she takes out the book. In a strange way, it is hers now. Toula has given it to her not once but twice. She opens it to where she was last reading.

'You must be ready to meet whatever is given to you and be ready to put possibilities into their proper place when they arrive. When things reach you, they will be in other peoples' hands, but seizing the moment and offering what is right and just in return, they will reach you safely.'

Niki turns right and across the road over to a small old building attached to the cinema on the far side of the library.

The door opens to a staircase and at the top of the stairs, Niki greets the woman who is sitting behind one of two desks in the sunlit room, which is mostly bare, with a few filing cabinets, a computer on each desk. Behind her, there are also double doors to the balcony at the front.

'Can I help you?' the woman asks, sounding a little bored. Niki has seen the woman many times around Saros but she does not know her name, nor had she any idea that she worked here.

'I wonder if the person who manages this office is in?'

The woman doesn't answer but points to a closed door to the side of her desk. Niki knocks and waits.

'Come!' a baritone voice bellows.

This room is also impersonal and official looking with aging wooden furniture and wall to ceiling shelving full of box files.

'Hello. I understand you have a vacancy.'

'No.' He looks up from the papers he is shuffling. He is not an ugly man but he has an unkemptness that suggests he is single.

Niki's cheeks flush with heat and the terse reply. Was Toula wrong? Has she been too eager to *put things that arrive her way in proper order*? Rocking backwards on her heels, she judges how many steps the stairs is to bid a hasty retreat.

'Oh,' is all she manages and begins to turn to leave.

'But we will have at the end of the week. Are you interested?' He stands and comes around his desk. He has dark sweat-stained circles under his arms and his forehead is beaded with moisture even though the air conditioning unit is blasting out cold air. 'The previous girl has not left, but you are ready to jump into her shoes?'

Niki's eyes grow wide. Her fingers interlink in front of her, twisting. What did the book say? *When things reach you, they will be in other peoples' hands, but by seizing the moment and offering what is right, they can be yours.* Something close to that, anyway.

'Yes,' Niki says before she has given herself permission to do so.

'Constantinos.'

'Niki.'

They shake hands.

'So, a little admin on the computer, a little coffee making. You think this is the job for you, do you then?'

'Yes.' Her voice again. A little quiver runs through her; her hands shake.

'No need to be nervous. All we need is someone who can take details.' He looks her up and down and smiles. 'But I will be honest. What we are really looking for is someone who can manage the foreign customers. I don't suppose you speak any more English than I do?' He lifts an arm to show the full extent of the sweat ring and places his hand on Niki's shoulder.

'I speak English.'

'Really?' He seems genuinely surprised.

'Of course, and I can read it, too.'

'Well, well.' He nods, then shakes his head as if she has accomplished something he has being trying to do for a long time. 'That's fantastic. Such a relief.' He releases his grip. 'Can you start next week?'

'Yes.'

'Okay then. With a bit of luck, this will be a seamless transition which will reflect well on me!' He laughs and with a look encourages her to join in. She manages a smile. When his mirth subsides, he says, 'Just see Katerina out there and she will take your details.'

Chapter 8

'So, it's a part-time job. What would be best for me would be if you did two hours three mornings a week. Although we are open from eight in the morning until two in the afternoon.' Katerina leans through the balcony doors to exhale her smoke. The hand holding her cigarette extends to remain outside.

'So if I wasn't to do Tuesdays and Thursdays, that would not be a problem?' Niki says through the glass door. Katerina has turned her head away to inhale on her cigarette.

'Sorry, what?' Smoke escapes her nose and mouth as she speaks. Grinding out her cigarette, she comes into the office and they arrange a rough schedule. The pay is not as much per hour as Toula pays, but there are more hours a week. Katerina tells her in a flat, lifeless voice that the job is a wonderful opportunity. Niki does not need telling; the excitement churns her stomach. It is only when she is sitting on the bus to return home that she does some quick maths in her head and it becomes plain that it will take three or four years saving all the money to send the boys to university. The energy that came from getting the job seeps onto the floor of the bus, where it stays with the discarded tickets, an empty fizzy drinks can, someone's school workbook, a pen, a gum wrapper, and a pink ponytail band. She doesn't look up until the driver calls to her to tell her she is in the village.

There must be a better way. It is not a matter of working harder. She needs to work smarter, be creative, as the book says.

As she gets off the bus, Vasso waves from the kiosk and she returns the gesture, but her arm is heavy and the wave lifeless.

Head down, she continues toward her house.

'What's wrong with you then?' Stella's light voice greets her. She lounges, legs elongated, toes tuned towards each other, on a plastic chair outside her eatery. Her slight limbs move easily, one hand over her eyes to shield the sun's glare. She has on one of her usual shapeless floral dresses and her shoulder-length, slightly frizzy dark hair is tied back loosely.

'Nothing.' To go into it would make her sound ungrateful for all she has.

'You want a coffee?' Stella asks, her hand on the arm of the chair, ready to stand.

'No. Stella?' Niki pulls out a chair and sits. 'Do you think that by focusing on something enough, you can make it happen?'

'Absolutely.' Stella swirls the froth in her frappe glass with her straw, lifts the straw out, and licks it clean. She is about the same age as Vasso, older than Niki, but she belies the years in both looks and actions.

'Seriously?' Niki asks for confirmation.

'Yes, seriously. You become focused and you see opportunities.'

'Yes, but if you want something within a certain time limit, how can you make sure that happens?'

Stella looks thoughtful. Niki likes this about her. She can be flippant and humorous, always full of life and ready to laugh, but if you ask her a serious question, she is always willing to take the time to give it thought, make the effort to give you a considered answer.

'I think that sometimes, you just have to go ahead with whatever you want and trust that things will fall in place behind you,' Stella says.

She could do that. There is still enough in the bank to buy tickets for her and the two boys to fly to England in September. Maybe she should just go ahead and buy them and trust that the money will be in place to pay their fees and keep them there. She has also heard that it is possible to look on the Internet for a place for the boys to stay. If she could line up some flats to look at before they go, then all they would have to do is choose. Something near to the university to keep the cost of travel to a minimum, something contained so they are not forced to make company with people they don't know, students who might not be diligent, or those that are just there to have a good time. If they get a self-contained flat with a kitchen, they will save on food bills, too. A week's food shop between them, if they are cautious in what they buy, could work out very cheap. She must teach them how to cook. They could take the Greek cookbook! Maybe she could even send food over, or maybe she could just take a huge suitcase of things Karolos has grown at the back of the second orange grove. Is this stream of consciousness what the book meant when it said, *If your mind is focused, then opportunities will come your way*?

'You know, I think you have a point.' Niki stands. She must get the boys to show her how to use the Internet before they go out. Perhaps she should start by making a list of the things they will need: pots and pans, duvets and sheets. They will have to get all that. Maybe she can post those things over, or maybe if they take an oversized suitcase each? She has a lot to do and Karolos will be in soon, hungry. 'Can you do me chicken and chips for four please, Stella?'

'Really?' Stella makes no move to stand. In all the years Stella has been running the eatery, Niki must have had a take away only three or four times, usually on one of the boys' birthdays. It is not that Stella's is expensive—quite the opposite—it's just cheaper to kill one of their own chickens and slice some potatoes herself. If she can save a handful of coins, she will. But just now, she feels different. The surge of belief that everything is going to work out is filling her with hope again.

'Yes, really. I think you are right. I have to take that leap of faith and just go ahead. I suddenly feel like I have too much to do to spend a couple of hours cooking.'

Stella is on her feet now. She looks into the dark cool of the eatery where Mitsos is managing to turn the meat on the grill. The sleeve of his shirt that is usually tucked flat into the waistband of his trousers is hanging loose and Stella goes in, strokes it smooth, and tucks it back in. He smiles at her and his look lingers until Stella has to point to a sausage that is burning. He turns it with the tongs and then kisses Stella's hair just above her ear as she leans in to him. Much as Niki loves Karolos, he would drive her crazy if they worked side by side all day long.

The stacked tin foil cartons give Stella a moment of struggle before she manages to loosen the top one.

'Is this about the boys going to university in England?' Stella asks as Mitsos lifts a split chicken from the grill and places it in the container. Stella fills in all around it with chips. 'Lemon sauce?' she asks.

'Yes and yes,' Niki replies. They will only need a frying pan and a sauce pan. Two plates, two mugs. It's not like they are going to need much more than two of everything. How can she find out if it is cheaper to buy here and take to England, or buy in England? Maybe that is the sort of thing she can look up on the Internet, too. Other mamas must have asked this same question. Someone must have answered it.

'There you go.' Stella offers the foil tray of food lying flat in the bottom of a large carrier bag.

'Oh, thanks. I didn't really need a bag...'

'It's hot,' Mitsos says.

'They are good boys,' Stella assures her. 'They will always be good boys whether they go to England or not.'

'I know, I know,' Niki agrees. 'I just want the best for them.'

Stella looks her right in the eyes and for some reason, the intensity of her stare makes Niki think of the last time her *Očka* held her gaze as the small bus pulled away from the square by the war monument on Shëtitorja Mentor Xhemali in Përmet. Her last day in Albania.

Chapter 9

The boys' laptop is linked to the Internet by way of a neighbour's connection. Petros assures her it is above board and that the neighbour knows, but Spiros shuffles from foot to foot. Niki decides it is better not to know the details and instead, she rearranges the kitchen chairs so they can all sit around one side of the table without the sun streaming in through the kitchen window either blinding them or making the screen impossible to see. In the end, she resorts to hanging a tea towel over the slightly opened window and the room falls into a mottled shade.

It is strange being taught by her sons, who for so many years, as they have grown, she has sat next to and helped to study, their dark heads bent over their exercise books. Now they tower over her in both height and knowledge. She watches their deftness with everything that flashes onto the screen and initially, she is sure that she is never going to learn, it is all so quick. Spiros encourages her to type something and after her initial hesitation, she presses a key.

'Mama, you can type in anything you like, press all the wrong keys, press them all together at the same time if you want, but whatever you do, you are not going to break either the computer or the Internet.' Spiros leans towards her so their shoulders touch.

'Yes, come on Mama. You are the one always saying that we will never know what we can do unless we try.' Petros pushes the laptop towards her.

They wait expectantly and Niki feels the sense of hope lift her again and she becomes emboldened.

'Apartments to rent.' Niki speaks as she types, looking for each letter. It is a slow process. The screen jumps and everything is different.

'There, that one, Mama.' Petros points to a small picture amongst the writing.

'What do I do?'

Spiros shows her and the screen is filled with larger pictures of the apartment.

'Oh my goodness.' Niki takes it in and then types in some specifics; the distance to the university, those without shared bathrooms and kitchens. Is seems as if the world is suddenly at her fingertips.

'Right, boys. I can see this is going to take some time. There is such a choice, but it doesn't need all three of us. I'll narrow it down to a few and then you can choose.' The boys are happy to be released. Petros switches on the television and Spiros opens his book and goes back into his bedroom, leaving the door open.

The cheaper apartments seem grubby and Niki quickly rules them out. The ones that look big enough to take a second bed and that are clean and near the university are at a price she believes they can possibly afford, with her new job and working at Toula's. How she and Karolos will afford anything to eat or pay bills is another matter.

She spends all of Wednesday doing nothing else but learning how to use the Internet and searching for an apartment in England. On Thursday, she goes to Toula's to clean and Toula tells her she has been in touch with Juliet and her first English lesson will be the following Tuesday. The weekend is spent entirely on the laptop, and Niki expands her research to see how cheaply, in England, she can buy the things the boys will need.

'The United Kingdom is going to be much dearer than the *laiki* in Saros,' she tells the chickens who are in the kitchen again. Karolos is at the *kafeneio* and the boys are still in bed, Petros snoring just like his baba.

She clicks the links and follows the breadcrumbs until she discovers that the superstore Aldi exists in the UK, and that things like duvets and sheets, pans and rugs are actually a lot cheaper in England, to her delight.

'So cheap,' Niki exclaims softly to herself.

'More people, Mama,' Petros says, sleepy eyes looking over her shoulder. She ruffles his messy hair as he leans over to peer at the screen.

'More demand. Economies of scale,' Spiros agrees just behind him, stretching and yawning loudly. Niki understands 'more demand' but she does not know what 'economies of scale' means, and she stays silent.

By the middle of the weekend, she has listed twenty flats that will do. After a quick read of the first two pages of the stolen book to give her an extra push, she is feeling so totally confident that it will all fall into place that on Sunday morning, she goes ahead and books the plane tickets for the three of them to fly to England in September and then goes on to arrange with the estate agents to see the best of the flats as soon as they arrive, and then realises she has not discussed any of it with Karolos.

It's time he knew what is going on, and maybe it will motivate him to ring the buyer again, pressure Tasso for what they are owed.

The boys have laid the table and the roast is out of the oven. Karolos comes in from the orchards and they all sit down to a lazy late Sunday afternoon meal.

'I met Yorgos in the village,' Karolos says, holding out his plate to be filled. 'He says that we would be better paying our national insurance through the bank.'

'Yorgos the accountant?'

'Yes.'

Niki puts his plate in front of him and starts to serve the boys.

'You might want to wait a bit for that.'

'Why? It makes sense.' Karolos eats hungrily without waiting.

There is no way to break things to him gently, so she might just as well say it straight out. But for the moment, watching the chickens pick up their feet and march in, heads thrusting, eyes alert for crumbs takes all her attention.

'You going to give me that?' Petros has his hand out, waiting for the plate Niki is in the middle of passing.

'Oh, yes, here.' Niki hands over the plate. 'Well, before you do, I think you need to make that phone call to Tasso who owes us for the oranges.'

'Niki, I am not going to ring him every day. There is no point. When he has it, he will give us the money. We have enough in the bank with the money from the mandarins to get by for now.'

'No we don't,' Niki says.

'Yes we do.'

'No. We. Don't.' She suddenly feels scared at how he might react.

'Why, what, Niki? What?' Karolos' fork hovers, raised to his mouth, temporarily forgotten.

'I bought the tickets to fly to England in September.'

This stops everyone eating, and the only sound is the click of the chickens' talons as they pick their way across the flagstone floor.

'You joke with me, right?' Karolos tries a laugh, but it doesn't really form. His eyes are wide.

'The boys going to university in England is not going to happen unless we make it happen, Karolos.'

'That is all the money we have!' Karolos puts down his fork. Petros continues to eat mechanically, as if he is watching television, looking from her to his baba as each speaks. Spiros puts down his fork, dips his chin nearer his chest, and watches them from under his brow as he sinks into his chair. Niki reaches out, fondles Spiros' hands, which are now on his knee, and pats them and gives them a reassuring rub.

'Well, you will have to get more then because it is spent,' she tells Karolos. Spiros picks up his fork but does not eat.

'And where am I meant to get it from?' Karolos pushes his chair back from the table, his eyes wide, the muscles in his cheeks twitching. He is handsome even when he is angry.

'Ring the man who owes us,' Niki snaps.

'He doesn't have it.'

'Well, neither do we. But at least we don't owe anyone.'

'We owe the National Insurance.'

'That's not people. Not like he owes us.'

'Oh Niki, why?'

'Because it's going to happen. They are going to England, so we will find a way.'

At this, Karolos shakes his head and looks at the floor.

She would like to tell him that she has another job. That she starts tomorrow. It would be a trump card to show that they must do all they can, anything they can to assure their boys' future. But Karolos does not want her to work at all. That is the unspoken way amongst the middle-aged village men. Their women don't work. It is a matter of pride, along with a sense of competition with their peers, who were once their classmates, of who is the best provider. She stays silent.

Karolos looks up from the floor and meets her, eye to eye.

'I cannot make more oranges grow, Niki my love.' He speaks with no energy.

'No, but you can get paid for those you do grow. You just need to be firm. And if you hadn't let your brother Grigoris take the land in the village, we could have sold it to a builder. That would have paid for the boys' education outright and we would be comfortable.'

Karolos stumbles at the change of subject. 'He needed the land in his name to get a bigger truck. You know they would not give him a license for a bigger truck without more land.'

'Yes, but it was only meant to be temporary. Why did you not insist that the land was signed back over when they had their truck?'

'This is all so long ago, Niki, you need to let it go. And he is my brother.' He sounds exhausted.

'Your brother and his greedy wife, they stole that land from us, Karolos. There is no other way to put it. Needing the land to buy a bigger truck was a con and it may have been long ago, but it is another example of people walking all over you.'

'The only person walking over me right now is you.' His voice is not rising. If anything, it is growing quieter.

'I am standing up for the boys, your sons, which is more than you do.' Her voice is growing hard, words cut off crisply. Her Albanian accent, which on a day-to-day level is unnoticeable, returns.

Karolos stands, gently moves his chair to one side, and with silent feet walks out into the sunshine, the chickens following.

'Any more potatoes, Mama?' Petros asks. Spiros' eyes are moist.

Chapter 10

'I don't know why they find it so complicated. The final figure is printed in black, in bold. It is quite clear.' Katerina points at the water bill.

'Ah, yes, but that is on the back of the bill. On the front, at the bottom of the breakdown, is one amount which is in red, but it seems that is usually a much higher amount than the real amount. How are foreigners meant to know the one in black is more important than the one in red?'

'Well, if they read it,' Katerina states. She seems bored by it all, almost cross that she sometimes has to make effort.

'I imagine they don't read Greek. That will be the problem,' Niki says.

'Anyway, here.' She discards the printed bill and turns to the computer screens. 'That page shows the estimated amount and if you go here...' The mouse moves from one screen across to the next and Niki feels as if she has just walked into a futuristic film. She shuffles in her chair, her neck craning forward a little to see everything that is displayed. 'That is where you will find the scan of the readings. The name is there.' Katerina points with her finger. 'So on this screen...' The cursor moves across again. 'Click here, and you can type in the name and their details will come up. Oh, and you can change to the English alphabet here, and then...' She types furiously, 'it will come up like this. Put in the number,' she types some more, 'and the computer does the calculation and the total comes up here. So this is what will be printed and sent out and then all you have to do is wait for them to come in complaining that they cannot makes sense of it. Coffee?'

Without an answer, Katerina leaves the room and Niki hears the sound of the coffee jar being unscrewed.

'No thanks.' Niki brings up the next screen and reads off the name. 'Are there that many foreigners here then?'

'There are quite a few in Saros and the surrounding villages, but the islanders come here to pay their bills too. Orino Island must be nearly all foreigners by now.' The sound of the electric frappe mixer drowns everything.

The bill processing is a slow business and Niki wonders why the meter man is not given some electronic gadget to type in the readings at each house so they are sent directly to link to the billing system. The scans of his handwritten forms seem antiquated after spending the last few days on the Internet.

Her hours pass quickly and before she has come to a satisfactory conclusion, she has to run to catch the school bus back to the village. Between Toula twice a week and this new job, she will be out every weekday morning. She likes it.

The orchards spin past and the soil underneath is light in colour, dry. Karolos will be complaining about the water pressure again when he comes home.

The following day, she is on the school bus again and walks down to Toula's. Toula has a new dress on and her shoes sit on the kitchen table where she has been polishing them.

'It is my first English lesson with Juliet,' Toula says proudly but Niki is distracted. One of the shutters has been opened and a shaft of light brightens the whole room. The daylight seems to subdue the ever-present ticking of all the clocks. There is no sign of Kyrios Apostolis.

'Oh, Apostolis is out,' Toula says, nodding in the direction of the open shutter. 'Do make sure that you close it before you go, if you leave before I get back, but I won't be more than an hour, so why would you be gone? What on earth am I saying? I think I am nervous, or excited!' Toula lifts the shoes to admire the glassy sheen in the light. Putting them on the floor, she slips them on. 'I just felt like being just a little bit rebellious this morning. It's more cheerful, isn't it?' She straightens and looks at the room bathed in sunlight. When she giggles, Toula sounds much younger than she looks, but as she laughs, her head wobbles side to side more noticeably than usual. Niki has come to understand that this is a sign that Toula is stressed.

'I will be sure to close them even though it looks lovely in here with so much light,' Niki offers, trying to sound calming.

'Yes it does, doesn't it? But do shut them if you hear the lift.' Toula picks up her bag and moves toward the stairs.

'Just the usual cleaning routine today, Kyria Toula?' Niki asks before she is out of sight.

'Yes Niki, just the usual. Oh, and the laundry needs putting away. It's on that sofa.' She points to the wooden and laced cane work three-seater with its oversized cream cushions. It has its back to the kitchen where the yellow table is laid, as always, with a fine breakfast. 'You don't mind having your breakfast alone, do you?' Toula asks just before her head is below the level of the top step.

Niki gives a little laugh at Toula's kindness and consideration. 'Have a good lesson, Kyria Toula.' And the old lady waves a hand and is gone.

After breakfast and having put the linen away, Niki is halfway through dusting clean surfaces and sweeping pristine floors when Toula puffs her way back up the stairs. Niki looks at the nearest clock. The hour has sped by.

'How did it go?'

'Oh, it was marvellous. Such a nice lady, that Juliet. I will learn quickly I think.' She takes a moment to catch her breath. 'It is coming up to my granddaughter's third birthday. I am hoping they will come here to celebrate. And as for little Apostolis the younger, I haven't even seen him yet. Two months old now!' Toula puts down her bag and wanders to a silver picture frame on the desk, of a baby being held by a very young child with curly hair and Toula's smile.

On the way back, the ground is dark beneath the orange trees and Niki breathes a sigh of relief. Once home, out of the burning sun, she reaches to take down the cookbook. She has decided to teach the boys three basic recipes each, to give them six between them for when they are at university. If they rotate the menu, they will not get too bored and they will at least eat well. She has told them there will be no fast food in England; the price of such things mounts up so quickly, they just won't be able to afford it. As the big old volume is levered off the shelf, the stolen book falls from its perch and nearly lands in the bin. Putting the cookery manual on the table, Niki rescues the embossed book and smooths the cover with fondness.

'You, my little book friend, somehow gave me the confidence to take a job I would normally have been afraid to take, dare to master the Internet and, last, and definitely not least, book tickets for September.' She pats the embossed swirls on the cover as if it is a faithful dog, then sitting down, she lets the book open at any page it likes and reads.

You cannot act in the past nor in the future, only in the now. There is no other time, so you therefore must act in the environment you find yourself in. This is where your wealth lies. Niki puts the book face down to ponder.

'Hm, really? So where is my wealth? Which environment, here?' She looks around at the stark room, kitchen one end, sitting room at the other, two pictures on the wall, one of her sons and one of Karolos' mama. 'It sure as anything is not here. So where? Toula's? She doesn't even need me for the two days I do already. And besides, cleaning, despite her generous nature, is not going to make me rich.' The chicken with the slight limp is at the doorstep. 'What am I meant to do, chicken, expand my thieving from Kyrios Apostolis' books to his clocks?' The chicken caws at the attention.

Then the chicken makes a burbling creaky sound that seems to go on a long time.

'The water board, you say?' Niki replies. The chicken ignores her. 'Sure. Just give me twenty years and I might make manger if Constantinos disappears in a cloud of smoke.' She closes the book and turns her attention back to the recipes. The boys can start today, learn and practice before they go. Green beans in tomato sauce. That's an easy recipe, and very filling. Petros can start today with that, using the beans that have been soaking in a saucepan in the fridge.

There is a layer of bubbles on top of the soak water, and she tries to remember when she put them there. It must be more than twenty-four hours so they will be soft enough. She sniffs the water to reassure herself that they are not fermenting. If she starts to boil them now, they will be ready for their sauce when Petros gets up. So in the meantime, she might spend a little time on the Internet. She has discovered a site where she can play games. There is a solitaire card game which she is getting quite good at.

Chapter 11

Learning her new job at the water board is not as hard as Niki anticipated. The office building itself is set into the steep hillside that limits the size of the harbour-side town. With so many buildings nestled in front, it catches very little of the sea breeze—even on the balcony where Katerina goes to smoke. It is another example of an old house converted to offices, the grand doorways and windows not so fine as those nearer the harbour with a sea view, but impressive enough. Attempts have been made to turn the elevated rooms with their creaky wooden floors into a modern workspace. Multiple sockets are available on each desktop, the wires hidden inside the table legs. But the wires from each station to the main socket snake across the floor, held immovable with layers of tape on the polished dark wood floor. Judging by the multiple colours of the tape, this system has been repaired and replaced often.

The air conditioning, which is constantly on at this time of year, provides a very welcome break from the summer's heat. But sometimes, the artificial atmosphere feels too much and she keeps a cardigan on the back of her chair.

'Oh it's so hot. The air conditioning does not work well, I think?' Katerina says. Yesterday, she complained that the air conditioning was too cold, and the day before that, it made the air smell musty.

She turns back to her work and sighs. 'It will make it easier for you Niki, if you do this part yourself, instead of backwards and forward between us.' Katerina passes a sheaf of papers with obvious relief and reaches into her bag for her cigarettes. Niki does not mind being given Katerina's tasks. Katerina's side of the work is more interesting, more than just plugging in numbers. She has to balance accounts, move things around.

The next Tuesday, which is usually a day she goes to Toula, the water board wants her in to do some specific work, so she arranges to clean at Toula's on the Wednesday. As soon as she arrives, it is clear that Toula is in very high spirits.

'I go,' Toula announces before Niki has even put her bag down. No breakfast is laid in the kitchen and two shutters are open, flooding the place with light. A free-standing fan is whirring away, the noise competing with the clocks, and a bee is exploring the sweet-smelling waxed furniture. The place feels so different for these changes.

'Where do you go, Kyria Toula?' Niki asks looking around. The place looks even bigger and grander in daylight. The polished dark wood floor has warped over the centuries, and it undulates now, reflecting light here, the shadow there. It is now possible to see that the table by the far sofa has warped to fit the floor and all legs touch the boards, unlike the sofa, which has three legs along its front, only two of which make contact with the boards. Niki smiles. At one time, such irregularities would have bothered her, as for so long she has hankered after, and valued, the modern. But the magazines on the rack at Marina's shop have persuaded her to reflect, and recently she has found herself valuing the old and even, sometimes, things that look a bit shabby.

'I go to England.' Toula says this in English.

'To see your granddaughter?' Niki says in Greek.

'Yes, I fly the day after tomorrow!' Toula flicks on the kettle in the kitchen.

'Wow, er, fantastic. So how long do you and Kyrios Apostolis go for?' Niki takes down two cups from their hooks above the work surface and the jar of instant coffee from the cupboard.

'No. I go alone.' Toula stands stiff-legged, her arms slightly out from her sides, fingers spread, palms towards Niki as if she has just come to the end of singing a song.

'Alone!' Niki cannot keep the squeak of wonder from her voice.

'I know! It's exciting, isn't it?' Toula relaxes her stance and takes the coffee jar from Niki and tries to undo the lid, but her twisted fingers don't have the strength, so Niki takes the jar back and twists off the cap for her and then reaches for a teaspoon from the marble draining board.

'He does it on purpose, you know.' Toula's voice is flat, her eyes on the jar of coffee. 'I say to him many times not to put the lid on so tightly. He knows my hands are not so good.' Toula's head begins to wobble side to side as she talks, the tension in her voice raising the pitch a semi-tone. 'But he seems to delight in doing it, so I have to ask him to help.' She sits heavily on a kitchen chair that matches the table, with shiny chrome legs and a bright yellow Formica seat.

'I'm sure he doesn't.' Niki pours the water into both mugs.

'No, he does. His game is to make me as dependent as possible. Always has been. When we first got married, we were equal but then we started the business together.' Niki frowns and Toula explains that just after they were married, they renovated the village house which she had inherited—and then sold it. They used the money from that to buy a plot of land that they built on and they sold that, each project getting bigger and bigger until they could afford to move out of Apostolis' village house and buy the big Venetian stone mansion they are in now.

'I did the accounts, you see,' Toula explains, 'and Apostolis quickly realised that I was the one who really knew the business. I knew how much we had, what we could afford, how to take out loans, I understood it all. He became the donkey, the work horse, the labourer. I did not mind, but he did. So he employed an accountant, took my job away. So I became a housewife and filled my days with my village friends. He complained a little that I was out a lot and that I should spend more time on the house, but life was not so bad. But then he saw this place.

Now, I have nothing to do but stay in the house. I have no friends here and ever since the accountant, I have to ask Apostolis for money, like handouts.' Niki understands well enough. She may have all the say she likes in the running of the farm, but the bottom line is that Tasso and the other orange buyers would no more talk to her about the oranges and mandarins than they would harvest the oranges with their own hands. It is a man's world. At least her job with Toula gives her just a small handful of independence; something which she, Niki, and no one else, has control over.

She sits and pours condensed milk from a tin into the coffees before pushing one towards Toula along with the sugar bowl.

'So, yes, I do think he does the lid up too tightly on the coffee jar on purpose, just so I have to ask him to help.'

'So, how are you going to get to England?' Niki stops herself. She was about to say, 'If you have to ask for money.' Even though she has worked for Toula for ten years, they are not friends in that way, and as the domestic help, she has no right to enquire.

Toula turns her face to the open shutter, the sun casting harsh shadow into the crevices and creases in her skin, showing her age.

'I was very brave. I went to the bank. And here is the funny thing: The bank manager is a cousin of mine, and so it was nowhere near as intimidating as I had thought it was going to be! He told me how the bank works and I find nothing has really changed very much since I ran the business all those years ago, not really, just a few small things. All the fear Apostolis had filled my head with over the years about how the knowledge I had was outdated and how complicated it all was is just not true. So I go to England the day after tomorrow!'

Digesting this news, Niki sees Toula in a new light. She can imagine how in ten or twenty years' time, this could be her, only she and Karolos would not have a big mansion on the seafront. More likely they will be living in the donkey barn. She snorts laughter at this thought and Toula turns away from the sun to see what has amused her.

'How long do you go for, Kyria Toula?' Niki turns the snort into a sort of cough before making this reply.

'Two weeks.'

Niki's shoulders slump. That's two weeks' lost money. Half a week's rent for the boys once they get to England.

'So I won't see you until the--' Niki looks at the calendar on the kitchen wall, the one with a large picture of a different clock for each month.

'I am back in two weeks and two days from now,' Toula chirps, her energy restored again.

'I don't suppose Kyrios Apostolis wants me to come in whilst you are away, does he?' Niki tries to keep the anxiety out of her voice and adds another spoonful of sugar to her half-drunk coffee.

'Best just leave it, I think. Oh look!' Toula points across the room. A cat has just jumped onto one of the sofas and is settling itself down. 'That cat is getting very familiar. He tries to get in every time I open the door these days.'

'Shall I chase him out?' Niki stands and takes her empty cup and rinses it.

'Oh, he might as well stay. After tomorrow, he won't have the chance to come in for two weeks.' Toula is smiling and, even though it makes the skin around her eyes pucker, she looks years younger.

Niki takes the things she needs for cleaning from under the sink and starts by polishing the desk where Toula keeps her silver-framed photographs of her grandchildren.

'Actually, do you know what would be really nice?' Toula says. Niki stops polishing to look at her. 'It would be lovely if you would come halfway through the time I am away. Let's say the twenty-third, and give everything a quick polish. Here...' She goes to the desk, opens the top drawer, and takes something out and hands it to Niki. 'Here is the spare key.'

Chapter 12

Karolos lies on the day bed.

'Are you not going to tend the trees today?' Niki asks.

'What's the point? Night after night, there is no water.'

'Have you rung this man, Tasso, who bought the oranges?'

Karolos wraps his arms across his chest and turns to the wall.

'I'll take that as a no then.'

'Leave me be, woman.'

Niki continues to clear the table of dirty plates and cutlery.

'How can I leave you be? I cannot do it myself.'

'If you cannot do it yourself, then be quiet.' He tucks his legs up as much as the narrow day bed will allow.

'If I could, I would. But this Tasso would not listen to me.' The last of the dishes clatter into the old, stained marble sink.

'And what makes you think he will listen to me?' Karolos raises his voice, unwraps his arms and turns over quickly, alert, sitting up, looking her in her eyes. Such animation is unusual for him but Niki holds her ground.

'If you nagged him?'

'Like you nag me? Does it work?' Karolos' voice is harsh.

'People do what they feel most pressure to do.'

'People do what they can do. If he does not have the money, he does not have the money.'

'He has the money, Karolos. He took the oranges and he has sold them. He will have sold them for more than he bought them for. That is what he does, so he has the money.'

'The money is gone, he tells me. He had other bills.'

'So he paid the person who made his life most uncomfortable first. That is why we will never get paid. You never make anyone's life uncomfortable except mine.' Niki is shouting now. The passion and pressure she feels inside are too much; her teeth clench and tears prick, making her blink rapidly.

'You think that?' He stands. 'If you really think that, you should leave. You should not stay with such a man.'

'Oh, for God's sake.' All her breath comes out in the one sentence. Even at times such as this, one look from him, the briefest of eye contact, and she knows she will never leave. The very softness that makes him unbearable to live with is what she values and loves so much when it is directed towards her.

'Look Niki, we have food on the table. There are those who don't.'

Niki looks at the remains of their lunch. With what was in the bank gone on aeroplane tickets and the water board paying her three months in arrears, they have been reliant on her money from Toula for weeks now. But Toula is away for the next two weeks. Today's lunch was salad from the back garden, eggs from the hens, and a couple of sausages and a chicken leg that Stella said she needed to get rid of when Niki dropped in for a coffee and a chat.

'We have two boys. If they do nothing to further themselves, the only living they will have will be the farm. They will marry, they will have children. Are you telling me we will have enough food on the table for all those mouths? Do you want your boys to spend their lives chasing people who won't pay for their oranges?'

The light in Karolos' eyes dims, his head sinks.

'Niki, leave me be.' His voice is small. He lies down again, wraps his arms over his chest again, and turns to the wall.

'As a newlywed in my thirties, I should not have to be doing such work. It is demeaning.' Katerina is complaining, as usual. Niki does not bother to mention that the whole country is struggling with unemployment. Eighty percent of the youth are without work. She tries to concentrate on the screens.

'I have told Costas that as a husband, he should be doing the best he can for me. I have told him that perhaps he should look for work in Athens. I have had enough of this tiny, backward little town.' With this, she drops her pen on the desk, lets it roll to the edge and onto the floor as she gathers her things to spend what will probably be the next hour having a cigarette on the balcony, only coming in to top up her coffee cup.

Niki wonders if Katerina needs the stolen book more than she does. What did she read last?

There is only now, so you therefore must act where you find yourself. This is where your wealth lies. Something like that anyway.

Now if Katerina thought like that, she would stop moaning and get on with things. Niki turns the phrase over in her head. She is going to have to think of something herself with Toula gone for two weeks. Maybe she can arrange for a loan against her wages?

A woman with bleached blond short hair, a red face, white knee-length shorts, a white t-shirt covering a large stomach, and plastic flower-trimmed flip-flops comes up the stairs from the front door.

'Ah, do you speak English?' she asks uncertainly.

Her entrance has brought a wave of heat up from the street. Against the air conditioned office, it feels comforting, soothing. Niki preparers herself to explain again the intricacies of the water bill.

'Ah I see,' the foreign woman says after five minutes. 'So that is the amount I owe?' She points with confidence at the printed number.

'Yes.' But Niki then stops; there appears to be an error in the calculation on the screen and it does not agree with the bill the woman has brought with her.

'Oh, thank you so much, my dear. I don't know why I can't just come in when my bill is due and just ask you what I owe and pay it. I am so grateful. I have been worrying over this bill for days. Here you go.' She counts out the cash. But Niki is trying to work out if there is an error or not.

'It is so cheap compared to England, you know.' A car beeps its horn outside in the sunshine. 'Oh, that's my husband. I told him I would let him know if it was going to take ages so he could find a proper parking space. He has just pulled up on the kerb.' She leans towards Niki. 'Parking on the kerb. We are becoming so Greek.' She whispers and giggles and then jumps as the car horn sounds again.

'Look the change is only a few Euros. Please don't worry. In fact, take yourself for a coffee. It is the least I can offer for all your help.' And the woman turns, leaving behind her the smell of fabric softener and sunscreen. Another wave of heat drifts up the stairs from the street as she leaves.

'Katerina,' Niki calls. Her work colleague stamps out her cigarette and comes in.

'Gosh it's hot out there,' she complains.

'Look here, look. There is an error?' Niki points to the screen.

'I don't see an error?' Katerina leans over Niki's shoulder to study the figures.

'No, the error is that the woman's printed bill does not match what is on the records. She has overpaid.'

'Ah well, never mind. Just put it in with the rest. The billing system is not reconciled with the deposits, and anyway, the account we pay it all into is not just for water. It's the central account for all payments made to the council. You know, I think I might take an early lunch.'

'That's mad! How can anyone keep track of anything? What about the accountant? How does he make sense of it all?'

Katerina laughs. 'Have you not met him yet?' Niki shakes her head. 'Cousin of Constantinos. Spends more time in there,' she points to the office, 'drinking whiskey and talking about old times. I don't think he goes into much detail with the accounts. He takes a quick look and signs it off. You want to come for lunch? I've had enough of this place.'

For Niki, there is something in that final sentence, in the tone, in the whining quality that displays all Katerina's ingratitude for the work she has. Having learnt most of what she does, Niki knows it is not a difficult job and that it is fairly satisfying. If she had Katerina's pay, it may not be enough to allow her to be able to sleep easy about the boys, but at least things would not be so tight. Since buying the plane tickets, she and Karolos have been unable to give the boys money when they go out. Who pays for them to get into the *bouzoukia* now? Who buys their drinks? If they are borrowing from friends, they won't have friends for long. Katerina does not know how easy she has it.

'Such a dump,' Katerina half-whispers as she gathers her purse and lighter.

Act in the environment you find yourself in. This is where you wealth lies. Those were the exact words, Niki remembers now. She turns from the computer screen to face Katerina.

'You know, you are right,' she says earnestly. 'You are so right. I think someone like you and your husband would be so much happier in Athens. You are so much more suited for city life.' Her sincerity shocks her as the lie drips from her lips.

'Wouldn't we though?' Katerina says, turning off her computer.

'If you are going out for lunch now, why don't you buy a paper, see what you can find for your husband up in Athens? Give him a hand?' Niki's forehead is cold; she can feel beads of sweat forming. What she is saying feels dishonourable and wrong and at the same time empowering. 'Do you have family you could stay with in Athens for the first few weeks?'

'Er, not really.' Katerina's shoulders drop but her attention remains on Niki.

'What? Surely a distant cousin, a friend of a friend?'

'Well, actually, yes, now I come to think about it.' Katerina brightens.

'There you go. Give them a call. Tell them you are coming.' Niki turns back to her computer and Katerina walks as if deep in thought, down and out into the sunshine.

'What are you doing?' Niki says to herself as the door clicks shut, and allows her head to slip into her hands.

The following day, Niki goes into the office early.

'Oh hello, this isn't your day is it?' Katerina asks from out in the sunshine, the balcony door partly open.

'No, I just thought I would get everything I was doing up to date. I still feel a little overwhelmed every time I come in. I just thought it would be better if I got ahead of myself.' The sentence does not come out exactly as she has rehearsed it but it sounds sincere, genuine.

'Oh Niki, hello. This is not your day, is it?' Constantinos comes out of his office and takes a new sheaf of paper out of the cupboard behind Katerina's desk.

'She came in to get ahead of herself.' Katerina comes in with the smell of cigarette smoke.

'Diligence, eh! Maybe you will rub off on Katerina,' he says with a laugh and goes back into his office with the paper and shuts the door.

Katerina snarls at the closed door.

'Malaka,' she hisses under her breath.

Niki ignores her.

'Look, he just took the last of the paper. Can you go and get some more?'

It is not a question. Niki hesitates. Is she expected to use her own money and when she comes back show a receipt, or will it be added into her wages when she gets paid? If that is what is expected, then she has to find some way of telling Katerina she has no money at all. She could say she left her purse at home.

'Here.' Katerina takes a cash box from her desk drawer and pushes it across the table. 'Just take what you need from there.' Katerina takes out a newspaper and opens it at the jobs section, which already has several circles around adverts. Taking a pen from the holder, she wiggles it between thumb and finger as she reads, ready for action.

'Where do I account for it?' Niki asks, taking out some change. 'Do I just put a note in the box of how much I spend?'

'What? No. It's petty cash. Take what you need.' Katerina doesn't look up.

'But surely I need to make a note somewhere?'

'Oh Niki,' she sighs. 'Sometimes it is so obvious that you are from a village. Why the fuss? Just get on with the job.' And with the hand that holds the pen, she makes a little dismissive sweeping movement.

Later, Katerina goes for lunch and Niki works through. The office hours are eight in the morning until two in the afternoon, by which time Niki can no longer find any more work to invent, so as a last resort, she tidies the office cupboard where she puts the block of paper she bought. She is just organising the last shelf when Katerina leaves and Constantinos comes out of his office to find only Niki remaining.

He looks out onto the balcony and, seeing no Katerina there, goes back into his office and closes the door again.

Chapter 13

The sound of goat bells drifts through the shutters with the early morning light and Niki reaches for Karolos, but he is not there. The day they argued and he wrapped his arms around himself and turned to face the wall on the day bed was the day he no longer slept with her at night. At first, he fell asleep on the day bed in the late hours and it appeared as if it was an accident that he never made it to their marital bed. But then, with the excuse of 'seeing about the water pressure,' he has taken to spending nights in the little *plithra* hut among the mandarins, where a straw mattress and an old coat suffice for a cover. He comes home to eat with the boys but never stays long enough to be alone with her. His actions force Niki to finally accept the truth, that he lives as a simple orange farmer with the little he has because he just cannot stand the stress that is necessary to be anything more. At first, this realisation shocked her. All these years, her belief made him fit the mould of one man, a man she needed him to be, but really, she now realises, he could not fit that mould even if he tried. She isn't so much shocked at him, because in her heart she has always known that this was the case. Mostly she is shocked at herself, at how her own views had blinded her and prevented her from seeing the core of who he is. Nor, she is also taken aback to find, is it difficult to partially agree with his stand. Wealth for the sake of wealth is just a lot of stress for no purpose. In fact, they would be fine if it wasn't for the boys. But she did not go through all she had been through—leaving behind her parents and Albania, her time in Athens, living hand to mouth, saving all she and Karolos could as orange farmers, not even being able to afford to go back for her parents' funerals, scrimping on little things here and there for years—to have her boys end up in the same hand-to-mouth trap. No!

His side of the bed feels cool to her touch and she rolls onto it, missing him. She would never have bought the plane tickets if she had known it would come to this, at least not until everything else was in place. And all because of that stupid book. That was what had encouraged her to take such a premature action. So what she has to deal with now serves her right. It comes from having stolen the book. Nothing good comes from doing bad.

There's not much time to dress; she must catch the bus. Today is the day they agreed that she would go to dust Toula's rooms.

She nods at the bus driver, a friend of Karolos'. They were at school together. Now he and Niki have an unspoken secret. When she ran out of money, she got on the bus and just told him straight.

'The water board pay is two months in arrears,' she said.

He simply nodded her on board and has not mentioned it since. She owes him.

She settles into her seat, scowling slightly at the smell of the diesel, and tries to open the window. Through the dust-smeared pane of glass, she can see Karolos sitting in the *kafeneio* at the top of the square, staring at her. He is unshaven and his hair has not been combed. As a reflex, she reaches for him, the still-closed window a harsh, unexpected barrier. Her chest heaves with the need for the safety and warmth of his arms, the tenderness of his love, the gentle sound of his voice. But to get him to return would mean giving up her dream for the boys' education, condemning their future to a hand-to-mouth existence.

Or, and her teeth clench with this next thought, grind away at the back of her incisors, or she can assure their future all by herself. Once their future is assured, Karolos will be under no more pressure. They can then resume normal life. How she can bring this about, she does not know, but she will do it one way or another. A small voice somewhere deep inside reminds her that she could not sink lower than the places she has already been and she looks away from Karolos to hide her shame.

Alighting in Saros, the slight bustle of the town fits her mood. She needs to be active, make progress, do something. Today, she does not take the back streets to the port, heading instead down the main road and turning off just before the water's edge, onto Toula's road.

Nearing the tall double doors, she fishes in her pocket for the key. It is a big old key, the ring large enough to be turned with two hands if necessary. It slides into the lock with such a satisfactory clunk that she pauses, almost tempted to do it again, when she hears a noise from inside, like a plea or a whine. Or is she mistaken? She stays still to listen, her hand resting on the key, ready to turn it. Maybe she was mistaken. She waits for the noise again.

'Ah Niki. Now this is a very useful coincidence.' The voice makes her jump and she turns to find Constantinos striding towards her. 'I was just on my way up to the office. Got a text from Katerina. Not coming in today. Need you. As I can officially call this an emergency, we can call it double time. Yes?'

'Er, I...' Her hand is still on the key.

'What was all that when you came in on your days off then, staying later than Katerina, cleaning out cupboards? I thought you were keen?' His tone is somewhere between teasing and condemning.

She looks back at the unopened door. She promised Toula, but then she could come tomorrow couldn't she? Why not?

'Okay. Katerina is leaving,' Constantinos says impatiently but in a confidential tone, as if designed to sway her decision. 'It's not official yet so... But she is. Going to Athens. She went up today for something or other and left me short-staffed. So I need you in today. And also, please get a mobile phone. If I hadn't had this luck of bumping into you, I do not know what I would have done.'

Niki's hand lets go of the keys and hangs by her side. Katerina is leaving! A hot flush rises from her neck. She feels a sense of responsibility, but then, isn't this what she had been wheedling for? This is the opportunity she was trying to create, isn't it? She feels a little lightheaded and overcome with a stream of thoughts that feel alien to her. Have the heavens sent this opportunity as a way out of her situation? Maybe she should go to church on Sunday and light a candle, say a prayer of gratitude. The more it all rolls around in her mind, the more obvious it becomes. Why would she have such a strong motivation to send the boys to university abroad without the world offering up some way of making her dream come true?

'I can do Katerina's job.' Niki swallows hard. Her pulse is in her throat.

'Well, you haven't been with us very long.' They walk briskly side by side. 'I think I would have to offer it out to...'

'No.' Niki stops walking. Her own behaviour is partly horrifying her, partly thrilling her, and the combination is causing her to suppress a nervous laugh. She could easily lose her job with this sort of attitude.

Constantinos looks the way he was walking and then back at Niki. Their halting in the middle of the street is not what he was expecting, and he seems keen to keep moving. Niki's hand covers her chest, to hold in the surge of power she feels there as she stays rooted to the spot. Unless he agrees, she is going nowhere. Her teeth are grinding away, so she forces them apart, opening her mouth slightly.

'Okay,' Constantinos snaps and they walk to the office in silence.

Chapter 14

Work is non-stop. Katerina is behind with so much of what she should have done that Niki struggles to catch up. Her concentration is disturbed again and again as one person after another comes into the office to pay their bill.

An old man who is hard of hearing and didn't have enough money to pay has just left and there are three files that need putting into the system when Constantinos opens the door to his office and emerges with a billow of smoke. Finding the coffee jug empty, he asks Niki to make some. Normally she would take such a request in the course of her day, but she knows that they have run out of coffee and so to make more means a trip to the supermarket by the bank.

'We have no coffee.' As she says the words, they make Niki cringe. She sounds like Katerina, seeing everything as an obstacle.

'Well, go to the supermarket then,' Constantinos says jovially, but with an edge to his words.

With a last look at the computer screen, to remind herself where she has got to, she stands. When she gets back, she must ask how to process refunds when the estimated bill is higher than the final bill. Also, Katerina's desk is a mess. She needs to go through the piles of paper and file them or bin them. The pale wood surface is not even visible.

'Oh, ah, yes, and whilst you are there, you might as well go into the bank.' Constantinos goes back into his office and returns with a canvas bag. 'You can deposit this.'

'Do you have a pay in book?' Niki asks, recalling that she has seen Katerina take this bag on a couple of occasions.

Constantinos laughs. 'How many accounts do you think the water board has?' He seems to think the request is very amusing.

'Oh, so the same one as...'

'Yes.' He is looking at Niki now as if he finds her lack of knowledge attractive. He glances up and down and pulls in his top lip behind his bottom teeth, releasing it shiny and wet.

'The petty cash is down to the last few Euros. There is not enough to buy coffee,' Niki says, fishing about in the petty cash box.

The phone rings in Constantinos' office so he returns to his desk, calling over his shoulder as he goes, 'Well, take it out of the sack, woman!' as if she has no sense at all and then he turns his back to take the call. He runs a hand over his hair, displaying the extent of the dark circle of sweat on his white shirt.

In the supermarket, with a basket of coffee and tins of condensed milk, Niki decides the office can afford a packet of biscuits. She is just heading for the checkout when it occurs to her that there is nothing at all left at home for the boys to eat. She didn't put any beans to soak last night. Payday is still four weeks away and it is still another week before Toula returns. The bag for the bank weighs heavily in her hand. No one keeps records and Constantinos is expecting her to withhold some of the money for petty cash. She could use a small amount of what is in the sack to sub her wage a little and pay it back in due course. No one would know and no one would be harmed. It would just ease the next week. It will feed her boys. The hessian bag scratches at her leg.

Her heart is racing as she heads to the checkout with the coffee, biscuits, lamb chops, a tin of corned beef, some slices of ham, a packet of rice, and a small loaf of bread. The carrier bag of staples balances out the bag of cash as she walks, one in each hand to the bank.

The queue for the teller is ridiculous. She takes a ticket that gives her a number, her allotted place in the queue, and sits in the only chair left, which is directly under the air conditioning and is colder than is comfortable. But she needs to sit. She must make a note of what she has spent, keep a clear statement of what she owes. Then, if needed, it is all written down. No one can accuse her of stealing. She is only borrowing.

The queue moves very slowly, each person having a drawn-out conversation with the tellers. Everybody knows everybody in this town and most are related like in the village, although more and more Athenians have bought holiday homes here in recent years, before the economy took such a dive.

Now only foreigners come to take advantage of the falling prices.

She waits.

The meat should really be in a fridge. She looks down at the plastic supermarket bag. It is not enough to feed the boys one meal, let alone for a week. If she is going to do this, she should really have done it and bought enough to last until Toula comes back. But at least this will keep them going for a couple of days maybe, if she fills each meal out with salad from the garden and bowls of rice or beans.

One of the bank's customers leaves and the number on the wall clicks over, beckoning whoever is next. There are still ten ahead of her. There are no pictures on the walls, nothing to look at. A sad fern wilts by a central column. It would not be a happy place to work.

Thinking about it, she might as well borrow as much as she needs. In fact, she could take out all that Toula usually pays her and then when she is paid, she can put that in the next bag to go to the bank. No one the wiser, and her week would be a lot easier. Yes, she will do that. Fishing in the bag, she comes out with a much larger bill than she was wishing for and is just about to put it back and look for something smaller when a tap on her shoulder makes her jump and in her guilt, she scrunches the note onto the palm of her hand.

'You the new girl at the water board? Judging by the bag, I must presume you are. Come through.' The thin man wears a suit, his jacket still on even though it is hot. He waits to lead her into an inner room. The sweat runs down Niki's back. He settles behind the desk and put his hand out, presumably for the bag, which Niki hands over.

'No need to wait when you come, you know. Just knock on the door.' He looks at his own office door to indicate what he means. 'Can't keep Constantinos waiting, can we?' He makes a noise somewhere between a chuckle and a scoff.

He counts the money and hands her a receipt and wishes her good day. The whole process is that easy.

By two o'clock in the afternoon, Niki is exhausted. It is partly from the work but mostly from the stress of doing what she knows is wrong. She keeps reminding herself that she is borrowing and not stealing, and for successively longer periods, her breathing returns to normal and she stops having paranoid thoughts. She makes a careful note of what she has borrowed in the back of an exercise book, which she locks in a desk drawer before she leaves.

That afternoon, Karolos comes for his midday meal with the boys as usual and raises his eyebrows at the sight of the pork chops. He eats with relish and a couple of times makes eye contact with Niki, conveying his enjoyment of his meal. He even, in a conversation with Petros, says something which they all laugh at. It is almost like they are a normal family again, until Karolos leaves, muttering about work on the farm.

Chapter 15

The following day, Niki pays the bus driver all she owes and a few coins on top, which he pushes back at her.

'It's life, Niki,' he says as if he understands her world and waves her on board. She admires his kindness. That part of the book is true for sure: The more you have that you can offer, the more good you can do in the world.

As she ascends the stairs at the water board, she makes an agreement with herself that she will go to Toula's after work and clean. It won't take long. But then she will need to take a taxi home. Maybe that is just the price she will have to pay for getting this new job. She cannot let Toula down.

She picks up the note that she left yesterday, reminding her to ask Constantinos what to do when a final bill is less than the estimated bill they have already paid. As the meter readings are only taken once a year, this is a common problem. The computer whirs into life.

'Niki, I have a few girls coming in today to apply for your old job. Can you take their details as they arrive?' Constantinos only opens his door a crack to deliver this request. His cheek is pressed against door frame and door. He has not shaved but the smell of aftershave percolates into the room as he closes his door again. Niki gets the impression that he has been here all night.

'Sure,' she calls out before the door is fully closed, 'Er, before they arrive, can you show me how to reconcile estimates to meter readings?' Niki pulls over the other chair to invite Constantinos to sit. He reluctantly comes to his office door, wearing the same shirt as yesterday, and stands behind her chair to peer at the computer screen. The smell of aftershave grows stronger. It is sweet and mixes with the odour of his underarms. As he leans over her and takes hold of the mouse, he pushes her forward slightly with his chest.

'Go here, click that, and their account number comes up. Click there, that's our account, type in the amount... Obviously you will have to do the calculation first.' He takes his hand off the mouse to push the desk calculator, to indicate how this calculation should be done. 'Click here and the overpayment is refunded directly.'

It is much simpler than she expects.

'And those who have paid cash?'

'That's why you need to keep the petty cash topped up.'

'Oh.' A momentary panic sweeps over her as she wonders whether she has kept back enough petty cash for this purpose. But she stays silent. There will be more farmers in today who will pay in cash. 'Do I print anything to go with their refund?' she asks.

His look silences her and Niki tries to pull away from under his arm but there is nowhere to go. His face is closer than she would like for comfort and his breath smells of coffee, cigarettes, and stale alcohol. A warm draft of air makes them both turn towards the stairs, where a young girl with long dark hair appears. Her long, painted nails click on the handrail as she comes up. She grips tightly, using the support to balance in her high heels.

'Am I in the right place for the job?' she asks and Constantinos immediately stands tall, pulling his jeans up under his hanging belly, and smooths his shirt down. Niki takes a fresh sheet of paper and asks her name.

By the time Niki has reconciled all the overpayments with the meter readings and the stream of hopeful employees have come and gone, she is exhausted but also refreshed with gratitude. So many people have applied for her old job; she hadn't realised how lucky she was to get it.

Constantinos endows her with keys for the office, tells her to get her own set cut, and locks up as he leaves early with the last applicant, a twenty-something who chews gum noisily. Once her desk is tidy, Niki walks to the bus stop without a thought for Toula, considering instead what to feed the boys and Karolos. Today she will make a risotto with the corned beef, one of Karolos' favourites. Maybe he will stay and talk a little. If he does, she will not push him, just ask how he is, if he needs anything. Does he even have sheets in the *plithra* hut? If he does, they will need washing by now. Poor Karolos sweats so much at night in this heat, he cannot be comfortable out there in the orchard.

'This is good,' Karolos says between mouthfuls. But Niki knows him well enough to know this is a question, and that he is wondering how she can afford to buy such luxuries as corned beef. Niki shakes her head. She never thought she would see the day again when she would consider corned beef a luxury.

'Katerina moved to Athens. I took over her job.' Best just be straight with him.

All three of her boys look up from their plates sharply. Spiros' eyes are a little wider than normal. She smiles at him, lets him know that it is nothing to worry about. Petros is the first to continue eating.

'Who's Katerina?' Karolos asks, his voice controlled, his fork hovering.

Her finger slips over her lips, sealing them shut, a reflex action that she masks by pretending to wipe the corners of her mouth. Her reality is that she leaves for work after Karolos is off to the orchards and is back before he returns for his midday meal. Surely it cannot be possible that she did not tell him about her part-time job, which means her full-time job is going to come as a slap in the face?

She could lie, say it is another cleaning job in Saros.

'Anybody want any more?' She gets up from the table with her plate, from which she has eaten little.

Karolos has always been old-fashioned. His wife in full-time work will be a stigma to him and will only make matters worse. But then, how much worse can they get? He is living on his own in a mud hut in his orange grove. She is sleeping alone in their marital bed and between them, a tin of corned beef is a luxury. She glances at him. He sits hunched over and in his eyes, she sees his knowledge, his belief that he is ineffectual, a failed husband, an unproviding baba, a beaten man. She hasn't the heart to humiliate him further.

'She did a temporary cleaning job near Toula's,' she mumbles. 'Water, anyone?' she adds breezily, putting her over-filled plate on the table and taking glasses off the shelf. Petros' hand shoots up as if he is in school, his mouth full of rice.

'Please.' Spiros finds his voice. Karolos nods pertly.

After they have finished the rice—Niki surreptitiously putting hers back in the pan so the boys can have seconds—Petros goes to have a shower and Spiros takes the laptop into his bedroom and closes the door, leaving Niki and Karolos alone.

'How are you, my love?' Niki opens as softly as she can.

'I am fine. We are all fine. It is only you, Niki, who is not fine.' He fiddles with a toothpick before putting it to his mouth.

It is so hard to hold her tongue.

'It's not for me. It's for the boys!'

'The boys are fine.' One arm over the back of the chair, legs stretched out in front of him, picking away at his teeth, he looks so content, but the tone of his voice tells her different.

'How do you know? Have you asked them?'

'Niki, we are all fine. We have what we have. We are lucky. It is only wanting what you cannot have that leads to misery.' He discards the toothpick on his plate. The sun is full in his face and his eyes are screwed up against the brightness. If Niki were to move to her right slightly, she would block out the sun, make his life more pleasant. But she doesn't.

'We are not powerless, Karolos!'

'And in your power, Niki, are you happy?' He shades his eyes with his hand.

'Will the boys and their future wives and their children be happy ten years from now when we all try to live from the one farm?'

'Will they be unhappy if they have each other?' He pulls in his legs and sits more upright.

'We can try,' Niki implores him, lowering her tone. It is better not to speak so loud the boys will hear. Although with the thin walls of the house, how could they not? It is also nice that he was stretching out in his own home, where he belongs. She should not have spoiled that. She offers him another toothpick, which he declines.

'We can only do what we can do,' he says. There is that edge of defeat again.

'There is no limit as to what we can do.' Niki tries to remain upbeat.

'That, Niki my love, is nonsense. We are limited by time and resources.'

'It seems to me that the only limit you have set yourself is the number of phone calls you are prepared to make to this man Tasso who owes us for the oranges.' The moment she has said the words, she moves towards him to retract them, stroke his shoulder, hold his hand, reduce their impact. Too late. He kicks back the chair and marches out through the door, chickens squawking in the wake of his invading boots.

Chapter 16

Niki peers between the laths of the shutters and watches Karolos stride across the square to the *kafeneio*. The bitter side of her snarls at him for him wasting money on coffee when she is scraping every cent she can get together in a full-time job that she must lie about for his comfort. But these thoughts are quickly banished as she reflects how stupid she has been. She could run out, across the square, tell him that she is sorry, ask him to come back, ask him to forgive her, let them start again. But by the time this idea has run its course, he is not only inside the *kafeneio* but sitting down and chatting to Cosmo, the postman.

With her nose against the shutters, she continues her vigilance as she ponders their situation. This year's oranges are not even grown yet, so they cannot be considered an asset. Last year's are sold to Tasso but not paid for, and there is no way to get him to pay. The mandarins are sold and that money has been spent on living and on the tickets. Perhaps she could she get a refund on those? But is that really the only option? If she keeps the job at the water board, the boys have a chance. She will get a month's back pay in a few weeks and that, surely, should be enough to pay a deposit on an apartment and part of the first term's fees. But what will they use to live on until then? And how is she going to lure Karolos back to her? If the boys do not go to university in England, will Karolos be secretly pleased? Or will he always know that he has failed them? If that is the case, there is no returning from that, a possibility she is not willing to encounter. They have to go! The bottom line is that she must get the boys to university by herself. If Karolos, meantime, wishes to spend his days and nights in a mud hut, well, forget him!

She steps back from the shutters. There will not be much available to put down for the fees. What if the university won't allow her to pay them by the month? They will have to! The boys have worked hard, they have got places, they are going. To hell with fees and Karolos.

But if they could get the money for the oranges, that would be the fees dealt with. The whole lot for both of her boys for a year. What if she went to speak to Tasso herself?

This thought is still rolling around her head throughout the following two days and all over the weekend. On the Sunday, it occurs to her that she does not even know where Tasso lives, so how will she find him to talk to him anyway?

`Sure, I could ask` someone else in the village,' she tells the chickens, throwing a second scoop of corn. 'Can you imagine Karolos' humiliation at me being his money collector?' The chickens continue to scratch and peck and offer no useful response, so she goes inside to start the evening meal.

Monday passes without event and the following day, she arrives in the office before Constantinos. Half an hour later, he phones in, says he is going to a very important meeting with some people from the mayor's office. If anyone calls, she is to take a message.

As she starts up the computer, she is shocked to see it is Tuesday, and that Toula is due back. She cannot for the life of her remember if she was meant to go to work for her today or not. Did they even arrange anything? Well, she cannot go. With Constantinos away, there is only her to man the office. She will go after work, say hello, and see if they can find time when she can still do her work that would suit them both better.

By mid-morning, three people have been in and paid their estimated bill in cash and she is up to date with everything on the computer. For the first time since starting the job, she has nothing pressing to do—until she remembers the new sheets of numbers the man who reads the meters dropped off yesterday. She can enter the data and sort out any overpayments.

She enjoys this task and occasionally, when she recognises a name, she feels a sense of satisfaction in giving her neighbour back their overpayments. She uses a ruler to underline the handwritten scrawl of the meter man as she works down the page. She stops at one point to take a phone call from an old man who came in the other day without enough money to pay his bill. He is worried his water will be cut off and what is he expected to do? Niki commiserates with his position but there is nothing she can do, nor can she advise him. She moves the ruler down a line and her mouth drops open at the next name. Tasso. There he is, with his address. Her heart beats a little faster. Now she knows where his house is. It is set back off the road between Saros and the village, and in fact, she passes it every day. It has four tall poplars, a tennis court that is growing weeds, and a Greek flag permanently flying above the two-storey house. Behind the house are purple fields that everyone in the village knows. These are the saffron fields, and the owner, presumably Tasso, Niki now realises, is said to have one of the only thriving businesses in the area, growing and exporting this expensive herb. Niki has never been sure what saffron is, or what you do with it, but if the fields belong to Tasso, he is definitely not a man short of money.

'And he withheld a few thousand Euros from us!' Niki stabs in the numbers and calculates how much he has overpaid. She will not give him anything back, not even if he is owed it. She looks at the calculator. So much? She does the calculation again. It's not as much as he owes her for the oranges, but it is a large sum. Perhaps she could talk to him? Demand that he at least advance her the amount of the refund?

But would he? Would he even listen to her?

The oranges are gone. He has no reason to fulfil his promise of what he agreed to pay. Even if they take it to court, it would be years before a judgement, and even then, who would enforce it? Tasso knows this, of course.

If she tells Karolos of the refund, would that make a difference?

Her fingers gently play on the keyboard, stroking the letters, not sure whether she will type in his name, click to pay him his refund or not. She knows she should. That is her job. But is this one of the opportunities the stolen book talks about? Her teeth grind away at the back of her incisors until, with her eyes shut, as if that makes her decision any better, she types in the surnames of her boys, Karolos' surname, her surname, the name this man owes an awful lot more to than this refund. She falters but before the anger subsides, she clicks and sends Tasso's refund flying into her own account.

Suddenly she is breathless. Her hands flop to her sides. What has she done? Can she undo it? But why should she?

No, what she has done is dishonest. She clicks various places to see if her action can be undone but can't find a way.

'*Skata*!' she whispers under her breath and closes her eyes, her hand rubbing her forehead. How is she going to put this right? If she tells Constantinos, she could lose her job. The only other person she could tell is Tasso himself. She could take the money out of her account in cash and hand it to him, explain her mistake, say it was a computer error. But that would be a bit crazy! It's possible that he could cause more trouble than Constantinos. Karolos is sure to hear. So is the whole village. The truth is that unless she tells someone, not even Tasso will know. It feels wrong and bad but unless she alerts someone, there is no one who is going to make a fuss. No one will find out.

No, she must do what is right.

With this thought, she takes a deep breath. She will lock the office for ten minutes, go to the bank, get the money, and go to the Tasso on the way home.

The rest of her morning is spent waiting for the minutes to pass until she can rectify her stupid, impetuous decision.

Chapter 17

Niki signals to the driver and he stops the bus, showing no interest in her change of routine. The gate to Tasso's house is a heavy steel structure that needs oiling, and Niki puts all her weight against it to make it move.

The path to the house is lined either side with flowers and the soil is dark and moist. Beyond, on either side, more flowers grow in borders and islands with walkways around them. The soil everywhere is deep in colour, as if it has only just been watered, or was well soaked overnight. No wonder his bill is so high.

The entrance to the house is designed to be grand, but age has decayed what once might have been an impressive façade. Now it appears pretentious. They say his wife died young. With her finger on the bell, Niki peers through the glass door that is reinforced with a swirl of metal work of stalks and flowers. The hall inside is wide, the floor tiled like a chess board, and a central curving staircase leads to the first floor, the bannisters the same metal work as the front door. She pulls her head away as one of the internal doors off the hall opens and Tasso himself strides over the pied floor to answers the door.

'Yes?' he asks without interest, clearly not aware who she is.

'Good morning, Kyrie Tasso. I am Niki, Karolos' wife.'

His eyebrows raise and if she is not mistaken, a twitch of a smile plays around his lips.

The sun is on her back and lights Tasso from his chest downward, the overly large Ionian-style porch shading his face.

'Yes?' he repeats as if they have no business between them. Surely he knows that he owes for the oranges? Surely his first words should be, 'I am so sorry not to pay you, Niki?' But his mouth is shut. He is waiting for her to say something.

'You owe us for the oranges?' she enquires, almost doubting herself in his presence. What if he says no? What if he denies taking the oranges? Surely Karolos has something written down, some proof? Why has she not thought of this before?

'Yes,' he replies, 'I have explained my position to your husband.' And with these cold words, he begins to shut the door.

Niki feels energy surge to her limbs, at this man denying her boys their education without even an apology or a hesitation.

'Er, Kyrie Tasso, has Karolos explained to you that my sons' education depends on us getting paid for the oranges?'

'He has explained everything, more than once, and I have explained my position in return. If he wants to talk more, tell him to come and see me.' The door begins to close again.

'Will we be paid before September?' Niki's voice comes out both at a higher pitch and slightly louder than she intended. Tasso's eyebrows rise again but he shows no sign of concern.

'If Karolos wants to talk, tell him to come,' he repeats.

'Kyrie Tasso, my husband is a mild and gentle man. People walk all over him and do not give him his due because he is meek and amiable. But his tender nature does not mean he does not deserve his pay or that he does not need it.'

Tasso starts to close the door again. She has clearly exhausted his patience.

Niki opens her mouth to plead Karolos' case further but her instincts tell her that it will do no good.

'Kyrie Tasso, before you close the door.' She puts her hand in her bag to take out the money and as it appears, Tasso freezes. She has his interest now, and her dislike for him grows.

'I wonder, Kyrie Tasso, whether not paying us was an oversight. A mistake?' His eyes are still on the money as she speaks. 'The reason I ask,' she continues, not quite sure where she is going with this, 'is that this morning, there was a computer error at work. I work at the water board, you know?' She adds some weight to this statement by looking around at his beautiful and well-watered garden, letting her eyes finally come to rest on the rich brown fields behind his house that will glow purple in the autumn when the saffron flowers are in bloom. His eyes follow her and his hand drops for the door, but he widens the distance between his feet and folds his arms to stand sentinel. She has his full attention.

'So this error... At least, I think it was an error. Perhaps you should tell me? This computer error happened when I typed in the numbers from your recent water meter reading. There was a difference between what you paid on your estimate and what you really owed.'

His eyes flick from the fistful of Euros she holds to her face.

'Now, I cannot be sure but I think the computer repaid the difference to the wrong account. I am not sure. If it did, the money could have gone to anyone's account. It could have gone to yours—or mine, for all I know. The thing about computer errors is you cannot know. But I have this feeling that you would not mind too much if it went to my account, as you have made a similar mistake in not paying us at all. Isn't that right, Kyrie Tasso?'

Her legs might give way at any moment and she has a ridiculous urge to laugh, or cry, or both, but nothing moves. She is stuck to the spot, everything frozen. Maybe she has gone mad and this is what it feels like? Do her eyes look wild, the white showing on all around her irises, or is she just hysterical? Will Tasso slap her hard across the cheek to bring her to her senses? Perhaps she should take a step back to be out of arm's reach. But no! She will not back down from this man who holds her husband's hard-earned pay. She stands her ground.

'I believe I understand you, Kyria Niki,' Tasso says, slowly taking in her words. 'Karolos was not so meek when he chose you for a wife.'

She is not sure if this is meant to be an insult, but all her efforts are being expended on trying to slow down her breathing, to appear calm, so she does not fully process what he has said. She puts her handful of Euros back in her bag and Tasso watches them disappear, a slight sad look in his eye.

'So.' He looks over at his well-tended fields. 'Am I to understand that these sorts of computer errors could make some sort of mistake with my water supply?'

As nothing of this kind had occurred to Niki, she is stuck for a reply and her mouth opens and closes without any words forming.

'Wait here,' he says, closing the door and retreating into his house.

Niki waits. It had never occurred to her that she has the power Tasso suggests. A car drives past the gate; its horn hoots as it overtakes a bicycle. The man on the bike waves, hand high in the air.

Niki feels exposed standing on Tasso's porch. If anyone sees her, how will she explain what she is doing there? And where has he gone anyway? Maybe he is calling Constantinos.

'*Skata*!' Niki is not usually one for swearing but on this occasion, she finds she can think of no other word. '*Malakismeni.*' What on earth was she thinking to come here? Isn't what she is doing fraud or extortion or something? Who is she kidding? It won't be Constantinos he is ringing. Someone like Tasso is bound to be friends with Saros Mayor, or the chief of police, or even the local judge! There will be no mercy. They will want to make an example of her, humiliate Karolos over his choice of wife, and highlight her nationality. They could even look into her past, expose her time in Athens. Is it possible she could go to jail?

She is just about to run when Tasso returns with a cotton-wrapped parcel.

'Last year's money. It is all there. I trust we are finished now?' Tasso's free hand is on the door again. Niki hesitates. It is on the tip of her tongue to say he owes for two years, but then that might be pushing her luck. He might condemn her for her greed and take back what he has given.

She looks at the small parcel. There it is: last year's money, in her hands, all neatly wrapped up. Her boys' future. Their ticket to a life more fulfilling than that of an orange farmer. The joy that flows through her brings so much energy to her limbs, she begins to rock her weight foot to foot and she decides to not jeopardise what she is being offered by asking for more.

Tasso thrusts the wad at her again and she takes it.

'We are finished, yes?' Tasso wants a confirmation, the twitch under his eye suggesting that he knows he owes more, that he is nervous.

'Yes,' Niki answers, fear squeezing her vocal chords so it comes out as a squeak and the door bangs in her face, and the resounding question that echoes with the sound of the closed door is: How will she explain this to Karolos?

Chapter 18

Alighting from the bus, Niki cannot suppress the feeling of elation that has been growing since her fingers curled around the cotton bundle and Tasso released it. The money is in her bag now and it feels satisfyingly heavy, nestled in the bottom.

'You look happier today,' Stella says as Niki approaches on her way home. She pulls out a chair from the table with her foot to offer Niki a place to sit.

'Had a bit of a good day so far.' At this point it occurs to her that she still hasn't been to Toula's yet, but right now she dismisses this thought as she just wants to savour her win over Tasso.

'Coffee?' Stella asks, but makes no move to stand.

'Sure.' Niki is about to put her bag down on the table and go inside to make them both a frappe but then pushes the strap higher up her shoulder so she can feel that money against her hip as she goes into the cool of the eatery.

'I can see Marina leaving the shop. She is heading this way, you want to make her one to?' Stella calls back to her.

The electric blender buzzes as Niki makes three tall cold glasses of coffee.

'You want one?' She asks Mitsos who is turning meat on the grill as usual.

'No thanks Niki.' And using his tongs he offers her a perfectly cooked sausage which she declines with a smile.

Through the door to the eatery's dining area where four plastic-clothed wooden tables and surrounding chairs jostle for room, comes the sound of farmers' laughter. Later today Karolos will be laughing as light-heartedly as that, Niki gloats, if she can find a way to tell him of their good fortune.

Outside Marina has made herself comfortable next to Stella, facing the road so she can watch the world go by. The square always has someone crossing it, sitting in it or gathered talking under the palm tree's shade, someone or something to watch.

'Kalimera Marina, how are you?' Niki asks, her voice light. She is filled with *kefi* - life's energy - and she would not hide it, even if she could.

'You seem full of joy. What's new?' Marina asks.

'Actually, can I ask both of you something?' Niki sits and draws her chair up to be nearer to her neighbours, her friends. They lean forward in response. Stella's eyes wide with anticipation, Marina, older than both of them, a little more reserved.

'In confidence?' Niki adds. Marina nods gravely.

Stella shrugs, 'Of course,' she says. In all the time Niki has known her she never has been a gossip.

'You know we were owed money for the oranges by Tasso?'

'Huh!' Marina says. 'Who isn't?'

'Really?' Niki asks. This is new to her.

'Owes us for the last two years,' Marina sighs, her features hardening.

'He owes a lot of people round here,' Stella agrees.

'I didn't know that. He owed us for two years as well, but I just thought that was Karolos being weak.'

'No, the man's a shark. Promised to pay me for last year's oranges if I sold this year's to him. He said he would pay it in one lump but I haven't seen a cent. So glad I have the shop because I don't know how you people who only have a farm can manage.' Marina gives Niki a sympathetic look.

'But you just said he owed you for two years, was that a slip of the tongue, did you mean owed or owes?' Stella has always been sharp.

Niki giggles, unable to repress her happiness. Stella sits up taller, puts her glass down and leans closer, reaching across to touch Niki on the wrist. 'Hey, woman, tell all? What have you been up to?'

'Okay, so here is the thing. I went and talked to Tasso.'

'Really?' Marina says.

'I've begged Karolos to call him, to talk to him, but you know Karolos. The man would give his last cent to someone if they told him a sob story. He makes sure he can do everything he can for everyone but not his own family.' Niki shuts her mouth, blinks hard, tries to say no more against Karolos. 'It won't help, and besides, he is a kind and good man really, it's just ...'

'Ah, men,' Marina interrupts.

'When you marry them you think you know them.' Stella nods, and Niki knows that she is referring to her first husband, not sweet Mitsos.

'Men and marriage, it's like being given a pig in a sack.' Marina laughs at her simile.

Stella looks at Marina sideways and her eyes light up, a giggle in the back of her throat as she sips on her frappe, waiting for Marina to expand on what she has said.

'You don't know what kind of pig you are getting until you open the sack and then whatever it is you are stuck with it!' Marina puts down her glass and rocks with laughter, back and forth as tears form in the outer corners of her eyes. Stella is grinning ear to ear and Mitsos comes out to see what all the merriment is about.

'Just talking about you dear.' Stella reaches behind her to tweak his apron at which Marina laughs even more heartily. Stella blows Mitsos a kiss and he bustles back indoors, colouring slightly.

The laughter subsides. Mitsos comes out with a few sausages cut up, with a toothpick stuck in each piece, but he doesn't linger. He and Karolos are not so dissimilar, but Karolos would never even think to perform so thoughtful an act.

'So, come on, we have distracted you. You went and talked to Tasso. You mean face to face?' Stella asks.

'I went to his house.'

'No!' Marina is old school. Still lost in a time when men did men's work and woman kept out of it.

'Yes!' Should she tell them about what she did at work? She cannot think of a way to tell it that won't sound bad. But she could alter it slightly, almost tell them the truth. 'You know he is the man with the purple fields? The saffron?'

Stella nods that she did know, Marina shakes that she didn't.

'Well I asked him, in a roundabout way, if he would like it if he didn't er... Well, if his flowers didn't grow, you know, if he didn't get paid for them, how would he feel?'

'And?' Stella asks.

'Well, I explained about the boys' future and how Karolos is so mild. And I said that does not mean he should not be paid and that we needed the money by September and he told me to wait. I thought he had gone to call the police or something, to have me thrown off his property! But instead he came back and gave me this.' She fishes in her bag and draws out the cotton bundle, unrolls it, and there on the table are the thousands of Euros Karolos is owed. A year's wage from the oranges. It is a sight that almost makes Niki cry.

'Oh my God. Put it away.' Stella flips the cloth back over the bundles of cash. 'Every man in the village will come begging from you if they see that.'

'Well done!' Marina says, her voice full of admiration. 'Can you go back and ask him for what he owes me now?' She laughs. Niki considers this and realises that she probably could, but says nothing.

'So your problem is?' Stella asks.

'The problem is, how do I tell Karolos that I got what he was owed without undermining him?'

Both Stella and Marina stop sucking on their straws, fall silent and sit thinking.

'Hm,' Marina ponders.

'Yes, well,' Stella contemplates.

'You see my problem?' Niki urges.

They say nothing, finish their frappes and sit some more.

'Okay, you tell him you met Tasso by accident... No, better tell him Tasso came to the house. Just keep it simple. He came to the house looking for Karolos to give him the parcel. Don't tell him what the parcel is, pretend you don't know. Then Karolos can tell you that he got the money from Tasso when he opens it. Simple!' Stella says with animation. 'All credit goes to Karolos.'

'What about Tasso?' Nikki asks.

'He won't say a thing,' Marina assures her. 'You think he is going to admit to a woman coming to his house and talking him into paying what he owes? He would never allow himself to lose so much face. No, Stella is right. Give Karolos the parcel and let him tell you what it is, and then all the male egos are kept happy.'

Stella splutters at this and Marina chuckles, and soon Niki is laughing the loudest of them all, mostly out of relief, the three of them cackling so much that Vasso's head pops out of the window of the kiosk to see what is going on.

Marina leaves first and when Niki decides she must go she takes with her a chicken dinner with chips and lemon sauce. The boys will not know what has hit them being treated twice in a week. She pays for it with some of the money that she took from the bank this morning, Tasso's overpayment, and considers that it is his treat - a 'sorry' she knows he will never say.

'Chicken and lemon sauce?' Karolos asks. He does not add the word again, but the implication is there, either that they cannot afford it or that Niki is being lazy not to cook for him.

'You don't like Stella's chicken?'

'No, no, I love Mitsos' roast.' His mouth stays open as if he will say more but he doesn't.

The boys join them at the table.

'Turn the television off. Petros.' Niki urges.

'It's the news, Mama.'

'Turn it off,' Karolos says and Petros does so with no further argument.

Right, she must tell them. She serves Karolos first.

'I had a visitor today.'

'Can you pass the salt please,' Karolos says. Spiros gets up and finds the cellar in the cupboard.

'Do you want the pepper?'

'Please.'

'You'll never believe who it was,' Niki continues.

'Is there bread. Who was it?' Karolos says.

Niki stops serving the chicken to unwrap the foil around the toasted bread that came with the chicken.

'Tasso.'

Silence. All eyes are on her.

'What did he want?' Karolos breaks the suspense. Neither of the boys moves.

'He was looking for you.' Does it sound believable? She puts down her own plate and gets her bag. Will he wonder why it's in her bag? If Tasso called round why wouldn't she just put the bundle on top of the fridge or somewhere?

'Did he say why?' Karolos' eyes have gone very dark, the muscle on his neck tenses.

'He wanted to give you something.' Niki retrieves the parcel and hands it to him.

Putting down his fork, he accepts it with both hands and pushing his plate to one side, puts it on the table and unwraps it slowly. The boys gasp in unison.

'There!' Karolos says quietly, obviously trying to hide his delight, 'I told you he would pay when he could! It is not good to be so distrusting of people, Niki.'

'Does this mean we can go to the UK?' Petros asks. Karolos stands, goes to the cupboard and brings out the ouzo bottle, which has just a trickle left in the bottom.

Niki gets four glasses and the spirit is shared.

'*Yeia mas*!' Their glasses chink. After lunch, and once their chatter has calmed, the boys pester Karolos for a lift into Saros. When they have gone Niki allows herself to enjoy the peace. She does not chase out the chickens until one of them grows brave enough to venture into the area of the room with the easy chair, the daybed and the rug, then she sends it flapping outside to join its friends. She waits for Karolos to return, feeling sure he will, but he does not come back immediately. It is much later, when Niki is tired and thinking about going to bed that Karolos opens the back door, comes in on silent feet, smelling of soil and the orchards. He takes her by the hand and leads her to bed.

Chapter 19

The following day, Karolos leaves for his morning in the orchards with kisses and tenderness and before Niki goes to work, she takes a moment to think through all that has happened. She is not ungrateful for the turn of events, the money, Karolos back in her bed, but she is aware that she now has secrets from him. She has never had secrets from him. Well, only about the unspeakable things she even tries to keep from herself with regards to the few months in her life when she first arrived in Greece. But these new secrets—her job, how she got the money, her dishonesty at taking Tasso's refund—makes it difficult to accept Karolos' caresses and kisses, his genuine displays of love, with her heart not feeling so free.

Taking down the stolen book, she hopes that she might find some answers between its pages. She reads from where she left off.

Wherever you are, you are in the right business, so take a look at where you are. This is not what she wants to read. She would rather learn something about relationships, not money, but she continues on. Maybe there will be a relevance. Besides, her bus does not come for another ten minutes and she is not in the mood to tangle with either the ironing or the dusting. With the shutters still closed, the room feels soft. Nothing is pressing.

'Act with all your heart. Do not daydream.' This sentence is underlined. 'Do not seek for some new thing to do, or some strong, remarkable, or unusual action to perform as the first step to getting rich. The source of your wealth is coming to you. You are attracting it to yourself. Listen to those around you more carefully. Maybe they have something important to say, some direction to point you. Everything that happens is a clue to how to behave.

'Above all, be prepared to take sudden and radical action if the opportunity presents itself.'

She closes the book and puts it in her bag when she hears the bus engine and hurries out to catch it.

The oranges trees flash past, the soil dry again. At this rate, they will get nothing for this year's oranges. The fruits will not fatten; there will be only a small harvest. Thank goodness the money from Tasso will cover the boys' tuition fees for this coming academic year. But if she wants to ensure that they can afford to stay for the whole of their course, she might have to press Tasso for the pay he owes them from the year before as well. Also, she and Karolos need something to live on. The struggle seems endless.

Settled in her seat on the bus, she takes out and opens the book to stop herself thinking, to tune into something more positive.

'The cause of failure is doing too many things in an inefficient manner and not doing enough things in an efficient manner. If every act is efficient and you perform enough efficient acts, you cannot fail to become rich.

'Once you have found success in one area, turn it to others. Every action is either strong or weak. Make them all strong, make them all meaningful. Make them all this way and you will prosper. Hold in your vision your end goal and by putting all of your power and faith into this, you will succeed.'

Well, that is clearly saying she should press Tasso for the money he owes them for the year before.

As they arrive in Saros, she feels energised by the words she has read and is ready to meet her working day. Perhaps she will even pass by Tasso and mention the rest that he owes them and judge how she should proceed by his reaction.

Before she has even sat down at her desk, she is hailed by a foreign woman marching up the stairs, demanding to pay her bill.

'I came here to retire, slow down. *Thello eimai siga siga*,' she gasps in badly accented Greek. 'But here I am rushing about, late to meet people for coffee. I had a bill, now where is it? Perhaps you know how much I owe?'

'Good morning. Please tell me your name,' Niki says.

She types in the woman's name and clicks through some screens on the computer to discover that the woman doesn't even owe sixty Euros. Before she can relay this information, Constantinos comes puffing up the stairs, engrossed in the local paper, muttering and exclaiming to himself. It makes Niki feel a little nervous.

The foreign woman takes off her sunglass, putting them on the desk to look through her bag for her purse, and extracts a pink bank note. Niki puts the note under the corner of a ledger and fishes in the petty cash box for the change.

No sooner is the door at the bottom of the stairs closed than Constantinos hurries from his office towards her, newspaper in hand.

'What, what is it?' Niki asks. A solid lump of emotion is rearing up in her chest. Is this to do with her? Has Tasso gone to the papers? The lump of fear reaches her throat and her temple begins to throb.

'You cleaned for Kyria Toula, right?' Constantinos asks.

'Oh my goodness, I forgot! I meant to go yesterday after work. She's back.' These new thoughts suppress her conjectures and she looks out the window down to Toula's house.

'Just as well you didn't,' Constantinos says, looking back at the paper.

'Why?' Niki stands next to him to look at the page he is holding open. There is a photo of Toula's house with an inset picture of Apostolis.

Constantinos straightens the paper with a shake and a pull and begins to read aloud.

'Toula Maraveyas returned home from visiting her family in London yesterday to find the lift in her house stuck between floors. When the electrician lowered the lift to the ground floor and the doors were opened, the body of Kyrios Apostolis Maraveyas fell out.'

Niki gasps.

Constantinos continues, 'The post mortem was carried out late yesterday afternoon and it revealed that he died of dehydration, having been imprisoned in the lift for the entire two weeks his wife was away.'

'Oh my God.' Niki cannot catch her breath and stumbles backwards, sitting heavily and holding the edge of the desk for balance. When had she been there? A week ago with her head to the door, listening to a strange sound.

'Oh my God,' she repeats. She can hear the sound again in her head; a faint noise somewhere between a cat meowing and someone weakly calling.

'Oh my God.' The words fall from her lips again. Why had she not opened the door? Why had she not put the words together in her mind at the time?

'You were there, weren't you, last week? Wasn't that the day Katerina walked out and you started work here?' Constantinos says.

Yes, that was why she hadn't gone in. She wanted the job at the water board, her chance! But at what price! Katerina would not have even left if it hadn't been for all the seeds she, Niki, had planted in her mind. All those suggestions that she would be happier in Athens just so she could have this job.

'Oh my God!' The words are muttered for a fourth time. She can find nothing else to express herself. If she had not been so greedy for the job, if she had been honourable and stuck to her agreement with Toula, then Kyrios Apostolis would still be alive.

'You look a bit pale. I'll get you a glass of water. Did you know him well?' Constantinos goes to the fridge behind the door in his office, where bottled water is kept to chill.

She had heard Apostolis and ignored him in her greed for this job, her determination to get her boys to England. When had the boys ever complained about being in Greece? When had they ever mentioned a desire to leave? Never. They have never even uttered one word to suggest they are not satisfied here, or that they are not content with a future as orange farmers. But then, when has she ever allowed them to think that they would become orange farmers? Those were more seeds she planted before they could even walk; tuning the BBC and CNN into their television, talking of the times when they would be at university in England if they worked hard enough. And they had worked.

And poor Toula. What's to become of her now she is alone? All because the promise of cleaning her house halfway through the time she was away was broken for the promise of a handful of cash.

'It is my fault,' she says.

'What?" Constantinos is reading the piece again.

'I was meant to go in and dust. If I had, he would still be alive.'

'Really? Then why didn't you?' He has turned the page now and is reading the sports page.

'I wanted this job.'

'What? This job? Here? Can you imagine dying for the sake of this job?' Constantinos laughs a dry, brittle sound. He has that about him—a cold, hard edge, so full of himself, he believes he should be important but without any of the skills to become so. There are rumours that he is trying to become leader of the opposition to oppose the current mayor of Saros.

Niki looks at him open mouthed, unable to understand why he is laughing.

'He's dead,' she hisses.

Chapter 20

Niki's mouth drops open, eyes wide, unable to believe Constantinos has made this last comment. But his words leave strong images in her mind: the lift that never worked, the lift she refused to go up and down in. The lift even Kyria Toula refused to use. Why on earth had Apostolis taken the lift?

'I am going out.' Constantinos leaves the paper on her desk. She knows him well enough by now to know he is going to the *kafeneio* in the basement of the town hall, to talk like old women with the other *businessmen* of Saros. No doubt poor old Toula and Apostolis will be the topic of conversation.

She sits at her desk and stares at a pair of sunglasses someone has left there. It takes a good few minutes for her to realise that they must belong to the foreign woman who came in earlier, and she tucks them in the top drawer of her desk. She will try to recall the woman's name and phone her, in a minute. First, she just needs to sit. Her eyes fix on something pink tucked under the ledger, pulls it out, and gazes at it blindly. Then it dawns on her that she has made another mistake. It's a euro note, a five hundred euro note, and she gave the woman change for only a hundred. One mistake after another, each because she is acting in haste or in greed. What kind of person thinks of getting a job over the call for help of a man stuck in a lift?

'How on earth do I tell Toula?' The corners of her mouth drag down, her chin wobbling as she holds the five hundred euro note between both thumbs and index fingers, stretching it taut, allowing it to fold, stretching it taut again. Her greed killed a man.

She pulls the note taut again and almost tears it.

How can the woman not notice that she only has change for a hundred Euros when it should have been for five hundred? The world is upside down. Those with money don't seem to need it, those who don't have it end up leaving people to die to get it. It makes her wonder if any of it really matters, once you are dead like Apostolis. His wealth did not save him and he won't care what happens to it now. Will Toula even care? She didn't seem to even talk to him. In fact, she always seemed a little scared of him. Maybe she will even be glad. At least she will be able to open all the shutters and let some light into her world now.

At the bottom of the stairs, the door bangs and the English woman who came in earlier rushes up.

'Oh, hello again.' Niki finds her voice. She feels to be performing without having to think, with a thin layer of unreality between her and the world. She can see herself, can function as normal but just at the moment, it all feels out of her reach. She continues to watch herself.

'Oh, hi.' The woman stops to catch her breath.

'Er, I was going to ring you,' Niki says and looks around for the five hundred euro note. What did she do with it?

'Oh were you? That was very kind of you. Didn't notice until I was walking along the harbour side. You wouldn't believe the trouble I am having trying to find a holiday apartment to rent in Saros. My friends are looking for something for the whole summer, May till November for the next few years, till they retire.' She looks at Niki hopefully, as if she keeps a list of such possible rentals at the front of her mind, but Niki does not hold the eye contact. She is still searching for the five hundred euro note. She would normally be feeling anxious in such a position, but right now, she is strangely calm.

'It's not as if I am the only person looking,' the English woman continues. 'I know a French woman who is looking for somewhere for her mother to stay when she visits. And I cannot always put up my own family, even. I just don't always have the room. So many of them visit at one time, and then there are friends, year round. Do you have a pen?'

Niki stops her search for the money to give the woman a pen. The woman then looks about the desk, so Niki offers a Post-it note.

'Here's my email address and phone number. If you can think of anywhere to rent, please let me know. I know lots of people who will fill it year round.'

Niki takes the Post-it note and, not sure what to do with it, sticks it to the screen of her computer. In the back of her mind, a vague recall of the book reminds her that this might be one of the opportunities it promised life would offer her, but Apostolis is dead because of the greed stirred up in her by that book and now five hundred Euros is missing. But still, there is no panic. She is floating free of her body and feels as if she has no part in any of it, watching herself standing there mutely, waiting for the accusation of theft when this foreign woman finally stops talking and finds out her five hundred Euros has been lost.

'Anyway, yes, I didn't notice until the sun was straight in my eyes! Then I remembered putting them down here.' The woman taps the table's edge and Niki realises she is talking about her glasses.

'Oh yes, your glasses.'

'Yes, my glasses.' The woman waits expectantly. Niki opens her drawer and takes them out. 'Thanks,' the woman chirrups and before Niki can say any more, she is trotting down the stairs, banging the door behind her.

Niki slumps into her chair, exhales heavily, and notices the pink five hundred euro note by her foot on the floor. She picks it up, looks at it, considers how meaningless everything in the world has become over the course of the morning, and slides it between the pages of the book in her bag.

'How's that for *being prepared to take sudden and radical action if the opportunity presents itself*?' she tells the slim tome. The floating feeling has not altogether disappeared, although she still has a sense of watching herself from the outside. She sits down to begin work.

The computer screen is hypnotic, the light drawing her in. Apostolis is dead because she wanted this job, Toula is alone because a lift didn't work, an English woman does not notice she has been short-changed by four hundred Euros because she is looking for an apartment and her sunglasses. Tasso paid what he owed by a threat he invented with power he imagined she had. The boys can go to university in England because of a book. The world of cause and effect has gone mad. Nothing seems linked to anything anymore.

'Just like the water board,' she says out loud as she breaks her stare and brings up the two windows that she must flick between to put in the latest meter readings. 'Why can they not make it so these accounts are linked?' she asks the machine as its fan kicks in as if protesting the heat of the day. Using the remote, Niki turns on the air conditioning.

'If it linked, I could do this and it would show up here.' She clicks to another window. Then she realises that she is about to do a refund for the lady who has just been in the shop. Checking the scanned, handwritten list of numbers, it seems the meter man has gone from one of the big houses on the side of the hill, just outside of the village, to the next. It is the slope that the foreigners like to build on because it has a view of the village, the plain, and the sea. Most of them have swimming pools or Jacuzzis and they all have big water bills.

So how does she make a note that this woman had the refund in cash? Her hands continue without her. Click, up comes the bill, tap tap tap, she punches in how much the woman should be refunded, click, her own account comes up. Enter. Done. She has just made another four hundred Euros.

With her head between her knees, she feels less lightheaded. Her breathing calms and her thoughts focus on her boys. Life can be so short. She could be hit by a bus, taken down by a heart attack, trapped in a lift and it's all over, having never known what life was like without the struggle, the endless eternal struggle of paying bills, having enough money to buy food and trying to give her boys the future they deserve.

Apostolis is dead and his book says, *make strong and meaningful actions to prosper.* Well, she will.

Lifting her head slowly, she dares herself to stand and flicks on the kettle to make a strong black coffee. Settling at her desk again, she sips the scalding liquid and then begins in earnest. The list of meter readings laboriously added to the computer records, the overpayments calculated and then, watching herself, she divides the number, half for the real customer, and half for herself, her own bank account on the screen, click click, enter. Another number, another foreign customer. Click click, enter. Another foreigner, click click, enter. A Greek, click, enter, an honest refund. Another foreigner? Click click, enter.

By the time she is due to finish for the day, all the new meter readings are on the system. She deletes the original list, switches off her computer, and as she tidies her table, she notices the Post-it note with the foreign woman's email and phone number. Taking it down, she puts it in a drawer, safely.

She is two thousand, four hundred Euros richer in the bank than she was this morning, and she has a crisp new five hundred euro note in her bag. Without too much hesitation, she takes a bus to the next town along the coast. It takes half an hour to get there. She climbs down to streets of unknown faces, a different community.

The bank is fairly busy and the teller has no interest in the account she opens, nor in the money she transfers from her joint bank account with Karolos to open this new account.

The bus back arrives in Saros too late for her to catch the one to the village, so she indulges herself with a taxi ride. At least she had the sense to change the five hundred euro note to small change, but even the twenty she hands Yianni the village taxi driver makes his eyebrows rise and he struggles for change.

'You are the first passenger I've had in three days,' he tells her. 'The downturn in the economy means taxis are luxuries now.'

Niki takes the notes in the change but waves the coins away. Yianni seems disproportionately grateful and she wonders just how bad things are for him. The book is right: the more wealth you have, the more good you can do.

Chapter 21

Karolos is not back yet. With the shutters still closed, the main room is relatively cool, the light subdued and the calm only rattled by Spiros and Petros, who are both gently snoring away behind their bedroom door. Turning the handle slowly and quietly just to look, she can see in the half-light that Petros is still in the clothes he went out in the night before, one arm and one leg on the floor. He is too big for his bed these days. The pine bed, with a thin mattress on a planked base, was given to him when he was so small. Spiros is curled up in a foetal position, a thin sheet over his hips, on a bed Karolos made from some packing crates that Stella was throwing out. Karolos sanded the wood by hand, long and hard, to get a finish he could paint so it did not look so homemade. It looks homemade.

Backing into the kitchen, Niki inaudibly unwraps and puts in the oven the frozen *spanakopita* pie she bought at Marina's on her way home. She could have made one but it takes time, and besides, a few coins in Marina's till are not ungratefully received.

With the washing machine churning away in the outhouse, an early small tumbler of wine in one hand and the book in the other, she goes out and sits in the shade of the donkey barn. They call it a donkey barn, and no doubt that was once its purpose, but it is now where the chickens roost and where they pile old hoovers, lamps and other items that have stopped working, and that Karolos has every intention of mending at some point.

The wine takes the edge off her nerves. The floaty feeling from which she has watched herself all morning solidifies and she feels more grounded. There can be no denying what she has done, but four things keep her from panic and shame. Firstly, the foreigners seem to have more money than they care to keep track of. They can afford to buy a house here and live without working, and will not even notice a little of what they have already paid out not being paid back, as there is no expectation of a refund anyway. Secondly, the water board will never find out—the system is too antiquated and there is no way of consolidating or checking. Thirdly, the customers have no way to know if their refund is correct or not unless they ask her and check it with the water board computer file which she has adjusted, so there is no reason why anyone will be alerted to her creative methods. And fourthly, she could die in a lift or under a bus or sitting reading a book by the donkey barn before anything is brought to light.

She takes a long slug of the wine.

The next part of the book is in italics.

'Put away weak and sickly thoughts and opportunity will spring up at every hand to aid your strong resolve. No hard fate will bind you to wretchedness and shame, as the good use you put your wealth to will clear you of all blame for what others could label greed.'

It is a long and drawn-out exhale that leaves her stomach sunk into her backbone. Her shoulders drop and she visualises the boys with black robes on and funny flat hats with tassels that the English wear when they graduate. A new life for them.

The sharp trill of the phone inside the house disperses her dreams and has her flying to her feet and rushing inside to stop the noise from waking the boys.

'Hello.' She tries to whisper but she is out of breath.

'Ah, hello my dear.' It is Toula.

'Oh Kyria Toula, I am so deeply sorry to hear of your loss.'

'Ah yes, not a pleasant way to go I expect, but then, he did insist on using the lift.'

'Are you alright, Kyria Toula?' Niki asks, aware of the lack of emotion in Toula's voice.

'Of course, dear. I'm fine.' She sounds sharp.

Maybe she is cross with her for not cleaning.

'Do you, er, are you expecting me, did we arrange that I would...' Niki does not know how to form what she is asking and be sensitive to Toula's loss as the same time. It is not as if life just continues as normal when you lose your husband, is it?

'The cleaning, you mean?' Toula asks. 'That is why I'm calling. You needn't come any more.'

There! It is no more than she deserved. Sacked! She should have gone when they had agreed. If she had, if she had kept her word, Kyrios Apostolis would still be alive and she would still have her second job.

'I'm so sorry, Kyria Toula. Can we talk about it face to face? Can we meet?'

'Oh yes, it would be lovely to see you. Come, dear, come. I will lay out a little lunch.'

With the oven down low and a note on the table to the boys and Karolos, Niki finds herself back in Yianni's cab. He drives keeping one eye on her through the mirror, his eyebrows raised. He asks her twice if she is alright but she has no desire to talk.

Toula is on the balcony, watching and waiting to throw the keys down. Niki does not mention that she still has the spare key.

The entrance is cold in comparison to the street, which is bathed in overhead sun, the bougainvillea cascading from every balcony. There is no way that she cannot help but stare at the lift. The doors are closed and someone has tied red and white tape around the handles to stop anyone trying to open the door. There is a curious smell, of bleach and something else that she cannot name. The sounds that she heard would have been coming from that lift. A whining like a cat crying, or a man dying? Oh God.

'Come up, dear,' Toula calls.

The stairs are dusty, which is to be expected, as she hasn't been to clean for three weeks now.

'*Yeia sas*, Kyria Toula,' Niki says formally.

'Come my dear.' Toula leads her into the main room that is so bright that Niki has to blink several times for her sight to adjust. Every single window and shutter is open. The sound of the traffic from the waterfront mixes with the quieter sounds of people walking along the cobbles and domestic life from the back windows of the apartments opposite. Inside, the place looks lovely now it can all be seen. But the strangest change of all is the silence within the room. Not a single clock ticks. Niki looks to see if they were all stopped at the same time, to show the passing of the dead.

'So my dear, I have laid a little lunch on here.' Toula points to the coffee table in the centre of the four overstuffed sofas. The best china plates and the silver cutlery shine in the sun. The effort Toula has gone to silences Niki as she is bid to sit. But she cannot eat any of the dainty sandwiches Toula has prepared. Her stomach is turning over and her mouth is dry.

'Kyria Toula, there is no way I can soften what I have to say. All I can add is I am so sorry.'

'What? Why are you sorry, my dear?' Toula seems oddly unaffected by recent events. Perhaps she is in shock. Apparently that can have strange effects. Or maybe there was more discomfort between her and Apostolis than she let on. But what about what Niki had promised to do and didn't? That would have saved her husband. Maybe this is how she deals with her anger, quietly, with containment and dignity. Toula won't have to say much to have her squirming with guilt at what she has done.

'I want you to know that I did come on the twenty-third as we arranged.' Niki starts to make her case, but she knows she has no defence, nor does she seek one. Her actions have left the gentle and kind Kyria Toula a widow.

'Oh my God. I completely forgot I had asked you to do that.' The skin on her forehead creases into a thousand furrows. Her eyes are bright, alert, and Niki senses that she is in panic. It doesn't fit. But the need to confess her own part in all of this is stronger than understanding Toula, so she ploughs on.

'I came but just as I was opening the door, I was called away.' Does she need to go into detail, tell of her greed for the new job, or is it enough just to confess her part in his death? But she is distracted as Toula exhales loudly, the smell of the coffee on her breath discernible. Toula's shoulders drop and a smile returns to her lips.

'Ah yes, well, these things happen. The place was not too dusty on my return. Do have a sandwich, dear.'

'But, and I am really really sorry, but I think I heard him, Kyria Toula. I think I heard Kyrios Apostolis call out and I ignored him. I was distracted by someone. Oh *Panayia mou*, Kyria Toula, if I had done as I agreed and come in to clean, he would not be dead. I am so so sorry.' And the tears that have been threatening since coming up the stairs now spill over and Niki finds herself lost in a strange mixture of grief and sorrow for Apostolis, and guilt and horror for some of her recent actions. It is as if all she is is falling into different compartments and the whole of her cannot be kept together as one unit. It is with some relief that she finds herself watching on, as if her crying has nothing to do with her.

'My dear, please do not cry. Please do not be upset. It would have been easy to have mistaken him for a cat whining.'

'But if I had done what we agreed, I would have been able to...' A new wave of tears comes. These are for Toula, who is now so alone.

'No, no, you must think no more about it. Life goes on. I am packing up this place and moving to live with my daughter in London. If you had come, these plans would have not been possible. So please do not be so upset.'

Niki finds her sniffles quietening at the calm sound of Toula's voice.

'Are you not upset, Kyria Toula?'

'We all die at some time, my dear.' She sighs. 'And he was not an easy man to live with, never fixing the lift but always using it. Every single time he had to go downstairs, he used it, making me worry. And always fussing over his clocks. The day I left, the taxi was waiting but still he was messing with his clocks. I was in the taxi ready to go, I was sure we were going to miss the train...' Her voice grows quieter and she stops speaking. Niki looks up from her lap to find that Toula is blushing bright red and busying herself with pouring coffee and spooning sugar.

'But he didn't take a taxi or the train, though? He was here?'

'No dear. Sugar? Milk?'

'Kyria Toula, how did you know the sounds I thought I heard sounded like a cat whining?'

The old lady looks up at her. 'Sandwich?'

Chapter 22

September comes more quickly than any of them expected. Suddenly their flight is tomorrow and the boys have made no effort to pack. Niki has been ironing for four hours now.

'Perhaps you do not need to fuss so my dear,' Karolos says. 'They will not have you to iron their shirts once they begin their lessons. They must learn.'

'Oh, and an ironing board. I have not written that down.' Putting her own iron down, she picks up from the table a sheet of paper covered in illegible scrawl and adds IRONING BOARD to the list.

'Did you go to the bank?' she asks Karolos. Her wages have come in and even though the amount is more than she expected, after doing some sums, she has found that it is only going to be about enough to buy all that the boys need to set up home. The orange money is enough for the first two terms' tuition fees for them both and with enough left over for a month up front on their rent. It does not cover their accommodation from when they first arrive until they have found a flat, and she hopes Karolos has not done the sums and therefore will not ask.

The list of flats she got the boys to print out at a friend's house is smoothed flat next to her list of essential purchases. The money she has taken from the account Karolos knows nothing about is safely tucked into a money belt which she has bought, folded up and hidden in her ablutions bag. Not wanting to draw any attention to her stash, she has only taken out enough to stay in a reasonable hotel for the seven days she will be there and have enough left over to eat out, as they will have nowhere to cook.

She has heard that some of the landlords want two whole months' rent as a deposit, so she has folded up a few large notes and hidden them with her underwear. She is ready for them.

That night, Karolos curls up close, his arm encompassing her.

'You will come back to me?' he asks with no hint of humour.

'Why do you say such things?' She snuggles back into him.

'I sense you have gone away from me a little. Sometimes I do not know where you go to.' His hot breath is on her neck.

'I don't go anywhere.' Niki can feel beads of perspiration forming on her forehead. She wriggles to be free. 'It's too warm to be so close.' She breaks free and throws the sheet off, but it is no cooler with no covers.

'You will be coming back to me though, won't you Niki, *moro mou*?' He adds the term of endearment he has used since their courtship.

'I have a return ticket, six days from tomorrow.'

'That is not what I meant.' At least, that is what she thinks he says, but his words are muffled into the pillow and slurred with sleep, and then he is snoring.

Niki lies looking at the ceiling, watching the shadows change. The eatery lights go out and the shadows across the room are elongated now, in the dim light from the one public streetlamp in the middle of the square.

The last time she left a country, it was from Albania to come here. Then she had a handful of sandwiches and a few saved coins. This time, she will go to a new country with more money than she ever dreamed of. The book was right: if all your focus is in one direction, there is no option but for that desire to come about because, let's face it, you are prepared to do whatever it takes to make it so.

Toula's face comes to mind and their conversation.

'Kyria Toula, how did you know the sounds I thought I heard were like a cat whining?'

'Sandwich?' she asked. The sun streaming in from the windows on three sides lit her hair into a candy floss crown. Her hand shook slightly as she held out the plate of sandwiches, and Niki took one automatically.

'I think that so much of our lives, we live because we are too lazy to make a change, or we believe the change will be too hard or we are scared to step into the unknown.' Toula took a sandwich herself and put it in the centre of her own china plate. She had cut the crusts off the bread and the sandwiches had been cut diagonally, into quarters, so each one was barely more than a mouthful.

'Mostly I think it is fear, don't you?' Toula commented.

Niki was not sure what was being asked, and she said nothing.

'Well I think that was me, anyway. I was fearful of what life would be like without Apostolis. Where would I go? What would I do? How would I make my money? And so I stayed. Year after year. You are married, aren't you dear?'

'I love my Karolos,' Niki affirmed.

'I am sure you do, my dear, but I am also sure there are many things about him which annoy you.'

Niki cleared her throat and drank some tea to sooth the tickle. She watched Toula intently, noting that she had lost the wobble that her head used to do when she was stressed. She was steady and still; it was only her hands that trembled a little to show her age. Did she know that Apostolis was stuck in the lift when she left? If she did, wouldn't that be murder, or manslaughter, or whatever they call it?

The next morning, they drive in the farm truck to Corinth, where the boys and their baba do a lot of hugging and hand shaking and Karolos has tears in his eyes and he waits with them on the platform until the train comes. As Niki hands up her case to Petros to take inside, Karolos grabs her and pulls her back to him.

'Niki, you are my love,' he says with such passion, she cannot doubt it. But she also hears within the words and the tone of his voice the promise that he is by her side to stay no matter what, and her defences spring into action. She feels accused.

'And you are mine.' Her words come out as a matter of fact and with a brief kiss on his lips, she skips onto the train.

The boys are on either side of one of the tables, their faces pressed against the window, waving to Karolos, who is smiling sadly but pretending to be happy and pretending the tears he wipes from his cheeks are fake, which they all know they are not.

Niki has not stowed her bag or sat down when the train moves away and from where she is standing, she can see Karolos waving long after there is any chance that the boys can see him, or that he can see the boys. He waves until he is just a black dot and he continues to wave as the train takes a long, slow bend and then he is gone.

'How long is the train, Mama?' Petros asks.

'An hour and a half,' Niki answers.

That is all the information either of her boys needs. Petros pulls his baseball cap over his eyes and his limbs become loose. Spiros bundles up the jumper that Niki insisted he would need once they get to England and uses it as a pillow, leaning against the window.

Niki didn't sleep well last night, with her thoughts on Toula, and there is no way she can sleep now. The orange orchards give way to olive groves, which in turn concede to fields of grapevines, stretching into the distance. Soon these are replaced with the oil refineries with their stench, and after that, they are in Athens, which seems to sprawl for miles and miles. The train grows busier and Niki becomes more vigilant, keeping an eye on their cases, which fill the luggage racks by the train's double doors. Soon she cannot even see the bags, there are so many people squeezing in and pouring on and off at each stop. Then, at the central station, the carriage empties and it is a relief to see the suitcases still on the rack.

'We there yet?' Petros asks sleepily, not moving his cap which covers his eyes. His biceps flex as he adjusts his folded, tanned arms. The English girls are going to adore him. He has her grandmother's blue eyes and Karolos' dark brown hair. He wears it like Karolos, too; short at the front and longer at the back. He took a picture of a nineteen-seventies footballer to the barbers to show what he wanted, thought he was being so different, and came back looking just like his baba.

She chuckles at the memory. Spiros wriggles, trying to get more comfortable. He is a more practical person, keeping his paler brown locks almost shaven in the summer. He too is tanned and muscular. Her little boys, all grown up. Men on the outside but still her little ones on the inside.

'No. Next stop is *Kifissias*.' His knowledge of Athens is as sketchy as hers, and the name of the station will mean nothing to him.

Athens thins out and is replaced by a shanty town, built haphazardly by the tracks out of plastic sheeting stretched over crude wooden frames and held in place with ropes. The makeshift houses seem to go on forever. She has heard of the gypsy problem, as they always refer to it on the news, but she hadn't realised the scale.

A warehouse with the word IKEA catches her eye out of the right side of the train. She would love to be able to look around, browse the cheap furniture, bedding, little things that make the house cosy.

Almost too soon, they are at the airport, and the boys are shaken, grumbling, from their slumbers and dragging the cases into the air conditioned terminal.

Chapter 23

The three of them stare, bewildered. They were prepared for England's wall-to-wall grey skies and endless drizzle, but the sun shines and the sky is blue.

'I thought you said I would need a jumper and a jacket.' Petros throws his jumper over his shoulder and wheels his bag toward the exit.

Niki is trying to put money back into her money belt. Already there have been unexpected costs. She was charged before she even got on board the plane because, apparently, there is a weight limit for the bags. Karolos told her not to pack the old frying pan, the olive wood chopping board, and two litres of olive oil, but it seemed a good way to save money once they got to England. However, with the amount they were charged, she could have bought all the items and more in the UK and still had change. Anyway, it is done now. Perhaps it is best if she keeps a tighter control on what they spend, better to be cautious. If for some unknown reason she runs out of cash, she has no way to get more; no bank card or cheque book.

'Okay. Let's see where we get a bus from.' Niki looks around at the vastness of the airport.

'It says trains this way?' Petros says helpfully, reading the hanging signs.

'I believe the bus will be cheaper.' Niki heads to a woman sitting behind a desk. Above her, a big placard says *Information*.

The woman, who more than fills her seat, is patient but obviously bored. She informs them, in a monosyllabic voice that, generally, the buses are a third of the price of the train but take three times as long.

'Five hours in all, but there are only three stations at which it stops,' she says, unfolding a map. 'Here, here, and here.' She points with her pen.

'Does the train stop as much as the bus?' Niki asks.

'There is one going in ten minutes that is an express, goes straight through.' The woman seems most pleased to be able to give this information.

Niki qualifies the price to herself with the reminder that she has exactly seven days—two to travel and five in which to get the boys into a flat, equipped for a year and enrolled on their courses. On the sixth day, she has a ticket to fly back, alone.

It will be fine. Everything is set up, with a list of appointments to see *digs*, as the estate agent referred to the rooms to let. Time, at the moment, is more of a luxury than money. The information woman explains where Niki needs to go to buy the tickets. 'You'll have to hurry if you don't want to miss it...'

'Are you sure we can afford this, Mama?' Spiros asks as they board the train. It is dirtier than Greek trains and everything looks old. Niki tries not to touch anything. The seats in front are covered in graffiti and Niki has a black line drawing of a man's genitals in front of her face.

'Sit here,' the ever-sensitive Spiros offers.

'When is the earliest you can enrol in your courses?' she asks the boys once they are settled and the train is pulling away.

'Mama, you have asked us this a hundred times,' Spiros says, his head moving as he watches the landscape speeding past.

'And I am asking again. Don't make this difficult for me. I have a lot of things to do and arrange and remember,' Niki snaps.

Spiros consults the papers from the university, which are looking a bit worn from all the times he has read and repeated the information to Niki.

'The earliest day is tomorrow. And the latest day,' he adds, pre-empting her, 'is in five days' time. Mama, you know this. That is why we have booked these dates.' His voice is soft and calm like his baba's. Poor Karolos. She should have kissed him goodbye. Why was she so cold?

'Yes, yes, I know, I know. I just need to hear it again. I need to be sure.'

'So do we enrol tomorrow?' Petros stops watching all that is passing for a moment to look at her.

'Yes!' Niki says. Is she really as tired as she sounds? 'Ten o' clock. We have an appointment with a Mrs. Appleson.'

'Mum, look how green it is.' Spiros points to a bank of trees that line a huge green field as the city drops away behind them.

'Cows, Mama,' Spiros says. There are no cows in and around the village in Greece. Goats—lots of goats—and sheep, but Niki has never seen a cow there. There were many cows back in the village in Albania. That seems a long time ago.

'Look at that river!' Petros' eyes are wide.

'I think that's a canal,' Spiros corrects him. 'Look, it's straight and the banks are flat.'

'Yes, but that doesn't prove it's a canal. It might be a river.'

'Look how even it is across and how straight-sided the banks are.'

'Boys, enough. River, canal...' Niki looks around the carriage, but no one seems interested in what, to them, must be foreign babble.

The green countryside becomes dotted with pretty houses which become more dense, then turn into bigger buildings, and they speed through a town.

'It all looks so unreal,' Spiros remarks. 'Did you see the buildings, all carved stone and grand?'

'Yes, but England was having an industrial revolution when we were occupied by the Turks,' Petros growls.

Niki sits back and watches the changing landscape, the voice of her sons becoming background noise. She has never experienced the world moving past her so fast before. The tracks beside them are just a blur. The fields pass one after the other, separated by green hedges and tall, bushy trees. The houses in the countryside are large and like storybook illustrations. It all feels too much to take in. Her eyes close and the train rocks her side to side.

When she opens them again, the countryside is flat as far as she can see and beyond the land, she can see the sea. It does not glitter blue as it does in Greece. Even though the sky is still cloudless and blue and the sun does reflect from the water's surface, the colour is a sort of browny-grey.

Spiros is asleep with his head resting on his neatly folded jumper against the window. Petros has his head back, his mouth open, the visor of his cap over his eyes. Outside, the fields are striped, neatly ploughed. Trees press up against the tracks and then clear just as suddenly.

'Next stop is Canonbury. All change please, all change... Next stop Canonbury,' an electronic voice tells her.

'Boys, Petros.' She gently nudges his leg with her foot. 'Spiro.' Spiros jerks awake, wide-eyed, alert.

'Petro.' He leans across the table and thumps his brother on his arm.

'Agamisou, what you do that for?' But Spiros is standing. Niki is in the aisle. The train judders to a halt.

Chapter 24

With much pushing and shoving, the boys manage to get the suitcases out of the rack and off the train. As the last of the bags thumps onto the platform, a man in a blue waistcoat waves a flag, blows a whistle, and jumps back on the train, which smoothly glides away.

'Mama, we are in a story like the Harry Potter,' Petros says in English and laughs. The station is solid and square but overhanging the platform is a roof, of which the facing board has been cut into deep zigzags, giving the place an unreal feel, as if it is a toy. The platform is crowded. The average age must be eighteen, and one or two mamas stand out, not so much for their age but by the look of concern on their faces. The youth have no such cares; they are all smiling or laughing or yawning.

'Welcome to the Hogwarts,' Petros continues. Spiros is arranging the suitcases so Niki is left with only the lightest to wheel along.

'Petros, take this one,' he says, and Petros is so busy looking around that he complies with no argument.

'Where do we go, Mama?' he asks.

Niki scans the platform for something that will help her to orient herself, but there is nothing. The people who got off the train are all cramming their way through a door in the big square building and Niki sets off to follow, finally spotting a sign marked

Exit. They pass through a high-ceilinged hall and then find themselves on a road facing ugly, angular new houses. The other people disappear with purposeful strides, the chatter and energy levels dropping away until there is just the three of them standing there. The world has a pinkish tinge and Niki looks at her watch.

'We are two hours behind here,' Spiros says and Niki adjusts her watch. It explains why she is feeling so tired. This is the time of day she would be putting her feet up, her chores done. They might as well just go straight to the hotel.

She wrote the name and the directions for the hotel down from the Internet in English, and she wishes she hadn't now, as she is too tired to struggle with a foreign language.

'Okay.' Niki pulls her small case. 'We go this way to a main road and then at the roundabout, we go left and then along a bit. It is about a twenty-minute walk.'

'Walk?' Petros groans.

Spiros says nothing, but he groans to himself.

'Well, this road, once we are past the houses, looks nice. There are trees.'

'There is one tree, Mama,' Petros says and no sooner have they set off than the main road and a roundabout are visible. As they keep walking, it becomes clear that the road beyond, the one along which they need to walk for twenty minutes, is a dual carriageway and there appears to be no path, or even a verge to walk on. It is much busier than any road Niki has seen back in Greece. It could be the centre of Athens, only the cars are not in gridlock; they are moving swiftly.

Petros stops and lets go of the handle of his bag, which comes to a halt on its little wheels and falls over.

'The wheels on this one do not work.' Spiros stops too.

'Come on, you two. This is meant to be an adventure. You telling me that you cannot walk for twenty minutes with a bag?' But Niki can feel her own resistance. Petros searches her face, curls back his tongue and whistles loudly at a passing taxi, which circles the roundabout and comes back for them.

'Come on, Mama. We are all tired; how much can it be?' Spiros says, opening the door for her. The driver is out and has the boot open and is loading in their cases before Niki has completely made up her mind.

'Where to?' he asks.

'Er.' Niki pulls out her notes and tells him the name of the cheap hotel the university had recommended on their website. They made it sound like a pleasant walk to the campus, but with all this traffic, how can walking be pleasant anywhere? It takes her two attempts to say the name with enough of an English accent for the driver to understand and then they speed away, merging into the dual carriageway with speed that scares her. The journey through three roundabouts—and all dual carriageways with no paths—takes no more than five minutes, but the charge is ridiculous.

'I don't understand,' Niki shouts over the noise of the traffic. The hotel, with its sharp gable end, looks like a house that has been extended with a large conservatory on one side of the new porch and a painted white wooden extension on the other. This last is tacked onto the front of the building and turns at a right angle to continue down the side. Its sloping grey tile roof does not match the red tiles of the old house and it all looks as if it has been cobbled together without much thought. But the paintwork is new and there is a sign by the bushes at the front that says 'Do not walk on the grass.' This is illuminated by a ground-level spotlight. More spotlights, under the grey-tiled roof, highlight long plastic boxes that boast pale orange and off-white flowers.

'Airports and stations,' the taxi driver replies. 'There is always a surcharge from them places.' He looks at the notes Niki is searching through to find the right denomination and fishes into his back pocket for a handful of change in anticipation.

Niki gives up a large note and awaits her change, which he gives her with a card.

'Name's Brian. Call me if you need a taxi. I can do a cheaper rate if you hire me for the day.' He grins warmly. 'Looks like you could do with a cup of tea, love.' With this he puts her small case under his arm, takes a suitcase in each hand and, without using the little wheels, he marches up to the door of the hotel and deposits them inside.

The boys follow, Spiros with the one other case.

'Brian,' he repeats with another big smile and leaves.

'Can I help you?' The girl behind the desk is all smiles.

Chapter 25

The room, which is described to them as a twin, has a double bed and a single and everything is maroon or cream except the sheets, which are crisp and white. Niki opens the narrow wardrobe to find a hanger for her coat. The door is only held by a hinge at the top, so she closes it carefully. The boys are tumbling about to gain dominance over the single bed.

'Don't be silly, boys. You share.' They leap from the single and push each other to decide who will have the side nearest the window on the double bed. Niki wouldn't care which side she slept if she had their energy.

Sitting on her narrow single, the small kettle and assortment of complimentary biscuits catches her eye and reminds her that the boys will need feeding. A menu under the phone has a selection of food that can be ordered via room service, and a separate list for the diner, as it describes the white, wooden extension that wraps itself around the building. The diner looks like a long white box with white wooden furniture. It looks more American than English to Niki, but then she wonders how much she knows about either country. Her references come from films and dramas that are repeated on television.

The cheapest plate of food is the same as a family meal would cost at Stella's. What she would give for Stella's chicken and chips right now, with lemon sauce and a glass of local wine.

'Mama.' Petros has taken control of the window side of the bed. 'I'm hungry.'

'Okay. We go; they have a diner.'

Apart from the food being bland and tasteless and three times the price she had estimated when she was back in Greece, the evening could pass without remark. Niki finds she neither likes nor dislikes everything so far. The countryside out of the train windows was amazing, all that green, but apart from that, it has all felt just a little bland, and very busy, as if everything and everybody is in a rush.

Both boys are snoring, softly, like they have done ever since they were babies. She listens to them and wishes that they will always sleep so peacefully, that their dreams will never be destroyed and that their sense of peace follows them wherever they go.

'I have a sense of peace now.' Toula had said. 'I thought I would be incapable, that life would swallow me up, that things would stop if Apostolis was no longer there, but instead, I find peace. The worst that could happen has happened. He died and I am still here. I'm still surviving. Not only am I surviving, but I am moving to England to be with my daughter and my grandchildren. That would never have happened in Apostolis' lifetime.'

'Kyria Toula, how did you know what I heard sounded like a cat meowing?' She had not let the question go. It horrified her.

'More tea?' Toula held up the teapot, steadying the lid with her free hand.

'Can you not answer me, Kyria Toula? Do you know how it sounds if you do not answer me?' Niki half-wished she wasn't asking these questions, but something drove her on.

'He had leukaemia, you know.' Toula poured into her own cup.

Niki can remember the sensation. Each of her limbs froze and her lips for some reason began to tingle as Toula's words made an impact. 'He was terrified of the future. What it held for him. Didn't give a thought about me, how I would be the one nursing him. But I guess that is what our marriage vows are for. To stop us running away when things get tough, to make us battle on in the times when we are really going separate ways.'

'So you didn't know he was stuck in the lift when you left?' Niki said quietly.

In the morning, the blackout curtains keep the day from entering the room and it is only when someone makes a light tap on the door that Niki surfaces.

'Sorry, sorry.' An Asian girl pushing a mop bucket, carrying a duster and a can of spray polish looks nervously at the floor as Niki opens the door. She begins to hurry to the next door along the corridor, the black liners tucked into the belt at her back crinkling as she moves.

'What time is it?' Niki finds her voice and her English.

'Sorry lady, really sorry.'

'Okay, okay. Time please?' Niki says.

'It is early. Eight, madam. I am sorry to wake you.'

'Eight!' Without another word to the girl, Niki shuts the door and strides over the carpeted floor on her bare feet, still with the presence of mind to notice how pleasant it feels in comparison to the cheap marble-chip floor at home. She pulls back the curtains and the English sun streams in, watery but bright.

'It's eight. Petros, Spiros, come on. Breakfast is included and I want you to eat until you think you will burst. But it is only open until half past. Come on, Petros.'

Spiros is pulling on his trousers, but his eyes are closed. Petros pulls the thin quilt over his shoulders and grunts miserably.

'No you don't. We have an appointment at ten and you have breakfast to eat. Up!' And with a yank, she pulls the quilt clean off him. He curls up tightly and groans but then uncurls, opens one eye, and is soon wide awake.

'Hey, England! I forgot we were in England. Come on, Spiros let's go see what the English have for breakfast.' Niki is about to ask them to wait for her but then she cannot see the point. If all goes well, in six days she will be on the plane back to Greece and the boys will be having breakfast by themselves every day.

With breakfast eaten and all of them back in their room, there is another knock on the door. Niki opens it with a smile, anticipating the Asian girl again, but instead a stout woman stands there.

'Nine o' clock,' the woman says.

Niki shakes her head.

'You were told, I believe last night?' The woman waits for Niki to remember but she does not. There is nothing to remember as far as she can recall.

'Canonbury Literature Festival? You not from round here, then?' The woman shakes her head. Niki mirrors the motion.

The woman sighs and her shoulders slump a little. Petros comes to stand behind Niki, curious.

'Canonbury Literature Festival. Biggest one in the UK. People from all around the world come. There are readings and talks; it lasts the whole week. The streets of Canonbury are just heaving.' This last bit of knowledge is delivered with a smile, as if this is the whole event's saving grace.

'Books!' Petros clarifies for Niki but at the same time questions the woman, who nods in return.

'So?' Niki says.

'So it is the one day of the year that we have to check out at nine o' clock. It is usually eleven but today is such chaos, it just gives housekeeping more time to sort everything out if we have that early start.

The girl on reception last night should have told you, and there were notices up on reception and in the bar.' She stops as if to think. 'You know, we have a writer reading some of her books here today,' she says brightly. 'We're expecting a big turnout. You're Greek, aren't you? You might like her; she writes about a village in Greece.'

'What are you saying?' Niki asks. Maybe her English is not clear enough.

'I'm saying you might like her.'

'No, about the check out.'

'Oh yes, check out at nine.'

'But I am booked in for the week. Does this not make a difference?'

'Oh.' The woman consults her clipboard. 'Not according to this you're not...'

'But I do the booking on the Internet.'

'When?' The woman checks her clipboard again and lifts up the top sheet to look underneath.

'Two weeks.'

'How did you pay?'

'Pay? I don't pay. I book the room for the week.'

'Ah, well, see, there's the problem. If you didn't pay, we can't hold a room. You have to pay and then it's booked.' The woman smiles brightly now and appears relieved.

'So I pay now.' Niki shuffles to get back into the room, past Petros and Spiros, who have crowded her by the door.

'Er, Madam, I'm afraid you can't do that.'

Niki turns. She swallows, blinks.

'Why not? I have money.'

'No, no, it's not the money. It's the space. People book us up months in advance. The people who have this room, Mr. and Mrs. Church, they booked a month. Everywhere in Canonbury will be fully booked for the whole week.' The woman watches Niki's face. 'Oh dear. Oh, I can see you have a bit of a problem. Tell you what. Pack up your things and bring your bags to reception and I'll see what I can do.' And without waiting for a reply, she clatters off down the corridor, the keys at her waist jangling, her pen tapping on the clipboard to the rhythm of her walk. She pushes the swing door at the end of the corridor with her solid hips and is gone.

'*Skata*!' Niki exhales.

'Mama!' Spiros sounds shocked.

'Don't worry, Mama. We'll find somewhere.' Petros is already trying to zip up his bag but he has not packed carefully and half his clothes are hanging out.

'Give it here,' Niki says and organises all the cases whilst the boys brush their teeth and comb their hair. They have a small bicker about who gets to use the hair gel first and Petros wins, as Niki could have predicted. She puts on her watch from the bedside table, checks all the drawers and the cupboard and once she is sure they are empty, she herds the bags into the corridor, the boys hurrying after her, offering belated help.

Chapter 26

It is a different girl this morning, and Niki tries to explain the situation. There is no room for them around reception and the girl asks if they could please take their bags outside, seeing as they are leaving? The reception phone rings and she turns her back on Niki and the boys. A laundry cart, white and billowing as it is wheeled past, catches on one of Niki's bags. The woman pushing it, in her purple gingham dress and off-white apron, puts her shoulder against the cart's frame and shoves all the harder, not looking to see what the obstruction might be.

'*Ela tora!*' Petros exclaims and pushes the cart backwards. The woman, although not slight of stature, staggers backwards and looks at Petros as if he has just slapped her.

'What on earth!' she exclaims.

'Your wheels were over the bag.' Petros holds up his hand luggage.

'I nearly fell!' The woman sounds offended.

'It is for you to look where you are going,' Petros retorts.

'I could have hurt myself.'

'*Ilithia Anglitha!*' Petros explodes.

'Petros!' Niki says sharply and he mutters an apology, also in Greek.

'Ah, you are here.' The woman with the clipboard appears from a door marked *private*.

'Agnes, push the cart round that way. Yes, there. Thank you.' She utters her thanks to Spiros, who is trying to help control the laundry basket, which is refusing to change direction on its caster wheels.

'If you put your bags behind here for a moment.' The woman points to a small space behind reception. 'Good. Right now, let's see what we can do for you people. Forget Canonbury; I can guarantee everything will be full. What about Whittlebye, up the road here?' She points towards the glass front doors. 'The next village along. There is the Royal Hotel by the sea. I'm not sure what you are wanting, but they are reasonable and comfortable.'

'Cheap, I want cheap.' Niki looks at her watch. They are going to miss their appointment. 'But we must be quick. I have an appointment at ten.' She pushes the letter from Mrs. Appleton—Admissions/Accommodation—under her nose.

'No Agnes, please don't wheel it back through here. Take the corridor that passes the kitchens,' the woman says as she glances at the letter.

'It actually says the woman will be there from ten, not that she will meet you at ten.' She taps her pen impatiently on the desk.

'That's good,' Petros whispers to Niki. 'We do not have to rush.'

'It's good not to rush,' Niki says. 'But if we do not have an appointment, will she take the time to see us?'

'Did you say cheap?' With this sentence, the lady with the clipboard brings them back to her focus and reaches out for the phone, makes a call in English that is too quick for Niki to understand. 'Okay, so they have one room left at the Gatehouse Tavern in Whittlebye. You have heard of the Gatehouse Taverns chain?' she asks but does not wait for an answer. 'The cost is less than staying here, but there is no gym.'

'Jim? Who is Jim?' Niki asks.

'*Gymnastirio*,' Spiros says in her ear.

'Oh, we no need Jim,' Niki assures her. 'How far this place?'

'It is not in Whittlebye centre; it is more this side, so you go left out of here.' She points vaguely at the front doors. 'Along the dual carriageway, and it is at the first roundabout, down off the road a little but you will see it.'

'So we can walk, yes?'

'Oh, no. You don't have a car? I can call you a taxi.'

'How much will that be?'

The woman stops and looks at Niki, glances over her clothes, at her bag. Niki straightens her top, smooths her skirt, and looks away.

'There is a bus every thirty minutes.'

Niki sighs quietly to herself.

'From where does the bus go?' she asks.

The campus seems like nothing but fields. They roll and dip with trees in between, the buildings themselves caught in the hollows or perched on the tops, magnificent architectural buildings in glass and wood. Niki has never seen anything like it, even in pictures. The only notion she has of what a British university looks like is from a calendar Stella once put up on the eatery wall. There, the buildings were the carved stone spires of Oxford, grand and imposing, only losing their magnificence as they were slowly smeared with chip fat and the days underneath were torn off, another month racing by. The next picture on the calendar showed a thatched cottage with rose bushes on either side of a black wooden door and a stream through the garden. One unbelievable place after another as the months become a year. But nothing like this, the real thing. It is so spread out, so open, so tidy.

Brian drops them by what looks like the university's main doors. He has been kind to them and after a small discussion, charges only five Euros more than they would have paid if they had taken the bus, and, he assures her, his taxi is twice as fast.

'There is a free phone number on the card I gave you, so if you need me... Have a good day, Niki.' He checks his mirrors and pulls away.

Inside the main entrance, a glass roof soars above them and the boys walk without looking where they are going and bump into one person after another with '*signomis*' or '*den peiarazis*' when the other person apologises first. Niki tries to keep focused but the happy-faced teenagers around them are clustering in groups or marching purposefully with a united feeling of hope and Niki suddenly sees all that the boys' new world could be. How far from her and the village they will move. The people around her are not struggling for every cent; instead they are making choices, carving paths to careers. Their very attitudes will take them where they want to go.

'Ah look, here is Mrs. Appleton's office.' Niki pulls at Spiros' sleeve and he in turns grabs at Petros. The three of them go through a frosted glass door on which 'Mrs J. Appleton' is etched.

Beyond is a corridor. Most of the doors are closed but there are some at the end that have queues of teenagers lining up outside. After some investigation, it seems Mrs. Appleton has the longest line of people waiting, and all appear to be foreigners. Some have dark skin, and Niki recognises Italian when a girl speaks to her friend, and someone else is having a conversation in her native Albanian. She looks twice at this boy and his friend, but he makes no impression on her. Maybe they are Albanians who no longer live in their own country.

After queuing for half an hour, Petros slides down the wall to sit on the floor.

'Get up,' Niki hisses.

'Why?' Petros sounds tired and is most likely hungry. It has been hours since their breakfast.

'You are not a gypsy. Get up.'

Petros slides back up the wall. 'You are in England now, Mama. You cannot distinguish between me and a gypsy. They call that racism here.'

'Are you being cheeky?' Niki is not amused.
'No, but I am hungry.'

Chapter 27

Finally, the queue moves. The Italians in front are in and out in a minute and Niki finds herself suddenly in the room with Mrs. Appleton, who is sitting behind a big desk with papers piled on every corner.

'Hello.' Mrs. Appleton smiles warmly. 'Do you have your admission slip?'

'Ah yes, yes. Boys, please your admissions slips. So I write to you on the computer and now I come. The boys, they need student accommodation, here at the university. Halls of residency.' Niki speaks with purpose. Karolos told her that she must sound as if it is a matter of course that Petros and Spiros should have accommodation with the university, 'Tell her what to do and she will do it. That is her job.' Karolos said.

'Like you have told Tasso?' she retorted and Karolos walked away.

'You applied online?' Mrs. Appleton asks.

'We are here now. We want to apply now,' Niki says. Despite Karolos' instructions to show authority, she can feel that this process is not going to be simple. She is so glad, and slightly smug, that she has taken the precaution of lining up appointments to see a number of privately rented apartments. A precaution that Karolos had had the cheek to call a defeatist attitude.

It is the brief silence before Mrs. Appleton speaks again that drains away Niki's small hope of rooms in halls for her offspring. Dismissing the idea before Mrs. Appleton does, she begins to wonder if they will be able to get to all the places they need to look at by bus, or on foot. They cannot really afford to take taxis everywhere, not even with kind Brian.

'Oh, dear, I'm so sorry, but if you have not applied online and been given a place, I am afraid you are too late.' Mrs. Appleton confirms what Niki already feels she knows. She hands back the admission slips.

Niki is already pushing the boys out the door. She must get the boys registered. Then they can start the hunt for somewhere to live.

'You can sign up to declare your interest in accommodation in case anyone cancels,' Mrs. Appleton says energetically. 'That's with Mrs. Bloom, in the room opposite.' She points out the door to another line of students waiting across the corridor.

'And where do we go to register?' Niki asks Mrs. Appleton as the next in the queue pushes their way in.

'In the main hall, you will find that there is a table set out for each course.' The smile is there again as she greets the next potential student.

'Petros, for saving time, you and Spiros go to register and I will sit here to say we want the cancelled rooms.'

'Where we go, Mama?' A flick of fear passes across Petros' eyes.

'The main hall,' Spiros answers.

'I will see you by the front doors when we have done.'

Petros puts his hand on Spiros' shoulder and they walk down the corridor. Two girls come through the door at the end, pretty, with long hair, laughing, wearing shorts. After they pass her boys, Petros makes a little jump, pushing off Spiros' shoulder and as he lands, he looks back at the girls but catches his mother's eye. His cheeks colour and then the door at the end of the corridor swings closed behind them.

Niki waits patiently. In Greece, all these people would be huddled around the desk. The idea of queuing patiently is so English.

'It's not fair.' The girl in front of her turns around.

'Sorry?' Niki says.

'The system. We are in the EU now, so why is it so much harder for us to get somewhere to stay than the English?'

Niki cannot place her accent. It is not Italian, or Greek or Albanian, or Romanian. Nor is it Croatian.

'I have explained that we just have to get a place because the fault is theirs.'

'Fault?' Niki asks, not sure that she understands what the woman has said.

'Yes. Now they tell me that if you register, you are liable for a whole year's fees even if you cannot stay because you can't find accommodation.' There are tears in the girl's eyes.

Niki can feel her own eyes widen. Her heartbeat speeds up, the pulse discernible in her ears.

'The British tell you everything that you must do with one breath, treat you like a child, but then expect you to know things you cannot possibly know. If they do not give me accommodation, I will take this to the Student Union, the European courts. I know my rights.'

The woman behind Niki tuts at the outburst. Niki looks at her.

'Is this true what she is saying?' Niki asks.

'*Nai*,' a voice further up the line rings out, from a boy the same age as Spiros, with dark hair, brown eyes. He could be nothing other than Greek. 'You Greek?' he asks in Greek. Niki nods, a short sideways movement of the chin, a very Greek yes.

'It is true, *kyria*. They make you pay once you are registered, no matter what.'

Without a further word, she breaks from the line of people and runs back down the corridor through the door at the end. Her hair falls out from where she pinned it up this morning as she looks about madly for the main hall.

Chapter 28

'Main hall. Where it is?' Niki struggles to find the words in English as she addresses no one in particular. The teenagers look at her, then look away, some laugh nervously, but no one answers her. She grabs the nearest boy by the sleeve. His eyes widen and his mouth opens.

'Main hall. You must tell me,' she demands. The boy's mouth opens and closes but no sound comes out and he resorts to pointing to a set of double doors at the far end of the hall, over the crossbeam of which in letters to the ceiling is written *Main Hall*. She does not have time to be embarrassed by her obvious oversight, and releasing the boy's arm, she runs as fast as she can to the main hall. The students part to let her pass, stare after her; their jolly chatter subdues and even Niki in her flight notices that the place has fallen silent and all eyes are on her. She partly does not care, but another part would like to tell them to all go to hell. How dare they stare and judge? They do not know her life, how things will be if the boys register but cannot stay. She bursts through the double doors to be greeted by an ocean of people milling around the many islands of tables.

Light blond heads, many light brown, some red, not so many dark brown. She searches for the boys' hair colour, but there are too many heads, too many people. She stares briefly at a shock of pink hair, then hurries, pushing past people with no apology offered as she approaches the first table. The plaque tells her this is where to enrol for Maths. She cannot read the sign on the next table: the words have many consonants close together, forming sounds that do not exist in Greek. She does not have the time to figure it out, but it is not Sport Science. She knows what that looks like written down. She pushes on, indignant comments ringing out behind her about her rudeness. The next table is not right, either. The girl behind the desk has a ring through her nose and discs in her earlobes.

In desperation, Niki puts her head back and is about to call her sons' names at the top of her voice when she hears the familiar melody of spoken Greek. Turning quickly, through the waving sea of people, she spots them and with elbows out, she pushes through the fray, calling their names. The glimpses she gets of them over shoulders, between heads, shows Spiros has a pen in his hand.

'*Oxi*!' She calls, but he does not hear. Turning sideways, she slides between a line of girls. '*Oxi*! *Stamata*!' She calls again. Spiros bends as if to sign. Petros turns to face her, his eyes scanning into the crowd. He heard her! '*Oxi*!' she calls again and, driving through the last few people, she grabs the pen out of Spiros' hand and pushes him away from the table.

'Did you sign?' she demands.

Petros is watching the people watching them. His cheeks have flushed and he gives her an angry stare.

'We are in the middle of doing it, Mama,' he hisses, trying to silence her. 'We are not late. We could not find the table.'

'Have you signed?' She pokes her finger in his chest, meaning him specifically.

'No! I am just...'

'You?' She turns and pokes Spiros in the chest.

'Now, Mama. I do it now.' He leans over the desk and asks for another pen but tutor does not move; he is staring at Niki.

'No!' Niki says and out of the corner of her eye, Petros melts into the crowd. '*Petros, ella edo.*' She resorts to Greek. He freezes but remains hiding amongst the other students.

Spiros stares at her.

'What, Mama?' he says softly, sounding like Karolos. Niki yearns for home, out of this madness, this dashing, this pushing. 'What is it?' Spiros' arm is around her shoulder and he leads her quietly away from the table, away from the stares. They are reunited with Petros.

'You sign and we don't get anywhere for you to stay, and we must pay!' she states succinctly.

'No worries, Mama,' Spiros soothes, 'We can register another day. It is allowed.'

Petros keeps his distance. As he is becoming more adult, he is also becoming more like her than he would like to admit, or that she feels comfortable with! It is like looking in a mirror, seeing all her bad points, her temper, her arrogance, her embarrassment of other people if they do not do things her way. Thank goodness his way is a different way, and that he does not also reflect her pushy side. If he did, she could imagine them falling out, spending time not speaking to each other. It would splinter the family.

'Eh, sorry Petros.' She tries to take his hand but he pulls away. 'You understand, I had to stop you.'

'So loudly, Mama?' is all he says and leads them out of the hall.

'Okay, we do something for you now, what you want to do? Tomorrow we have appointments all day to look at flats, but today we could have a happy day. We can be tourists.'

But Petros is not to be soothed.

'You hungry?' Niki asks.

'I'm starving,' Spiros answers. Petros is looking the other way, at a girl with blond hair piled on her head in a very messy fashion. She is slim and tall and looks back at Petros.

Spiros laughs at him and Petros, with a movement of his head, tells his brother that he should look too, but he has already spotted the attraction and they openly admire the girl who, instead of blushing, as Niki would have expected, smiles and waves. The boys' heads lean together and Petros mumbles something which makes them both laugh.

Niki looks around. A man in a tweed jacket is walking out of a door with a plastic cup. Through the door, it looks like there could be a cafeteria.

'Hey boys, come. We eat,' Niki says. The boys push themselves away from the wall they are leaning against with their shoulders, their movements designed to be watched, the two of them the perfect combination of Karolos when he was their age. So handsome, so young. She wishes he was here now, just to take some of the strain. She only left Athens yesterday and already she is exhausted.

'Please, please. Tomorrow, let us find a place to stay easily, no hassle, no worries, very cheap' she says out loud.

'What, Mama?' Ever attentive Spiros is beside her now.

The cafeteria food is bland but filling. Niki makes a joke to herself that it fills the insides but empties her purse. She doesn't laugh at her own joke. If the cost of things carries on at this rate and the flat they find requires two months' rent in advance, they might struggle. As it is, if she has to find the tuition fees for the whole year for the boys, she is going to have to find a way to transfer money from her own account back in Greece. She has no idea how to do this, but she will cross that bridge when she comes to it.

'What time is it?' she says out loud and looks at her own watch. 'Oh, is that Greek time or English time?' She twists her wrist to show it to Spiros.

'English, Mama.'

'Really, where have the hours gone?' It might be a good idea to try and move some of the appointments to see flats to today. 'It is late. What time do the shops open in the evenings here?'

Petros laughs, but not unkindly. '*Mama mou.*' It is his turn to sound like Karolos. 'They do not. They open at nine and stay open all day until five. Then they close.'

'They do not open in the evening?'

'No.'

'So how do the people who work all day do their shopping?' Surely he is teasing her. It makes no sense.

'No, seriously, they close at five.'

Niki looks at her watch again. It is half past four. So that is it, their day is done; there is nothing more they can do? It is a complete waste of a day. They have achieved nothing. She has learnt that she should have applied for lodgings at the halls of residency between the fifteenth of August, when Spiros got his results, and the twenty-first, the cut-off day, and that if they register but do not attend, she is liable for a year's tuition fees. That is the total result of all today's efforts. She leans her head on Spiros' shoulder, which feels solid, young, and vibrant. In comparison, she feels old and tired and lifeless.

'Maybe we should go back to the hotel and sleep,' he suggests.

'Oh yes.' Niki opens her eyes, suddenly aware they had closed, to find that she and Spiros are alone at the table. She sits up, her mothering instinct heightened, and looks around for Petros. He is sitting two tables away, his feet outstretched, his ankles crossed as if at home, his arm over the back of the seat next to him in which sits the girl from earlier, the one with the long blond hair. Her instincts tell her to go over, pull him back, ask him what he is doing. He doesn't know who this girl is, or anything about her. He is here to go to university not, not... Not what? Not have a life, not start a new life, not have friends, not have girlfriends, not find his life partner? But isn't that exactly why they are here? To give them new lives.

It hurts to watch him, so mature, in no need of her, so sure of himself. But isn't that also what she has always stressed in the way she mothered him? To the outside world, she might have seemed a little cold, a little harsh, maybe to some even uncaring, but she cannot deny her success. All she ever wanted was to give the boys the belief that they could survive independently of her and Karolos, the confidence to stand on their own two feet and not get into trouble. She never wanted them going out into the world as naïve as she was. For years, she hated her parents for not loving her enough to keep her at home with them, but when that hate grew so acid it burned inside, it eventually changed to bitter pitying for them that they were not wise enough to teach her not to love either, but to be independent and ready for the world and all she would come across in it.

Independence. That has always been her focus.

'Independence,' Toula had said. 'That is what we both wanted. I wanted independence from him, not necessarily to live without him, but just to stop being forced to be so dependent on him. And he wanted independence in everything. As he got older and had fewer things in his life, the one big thing he had left was dying, so he became obsessed with dying on his own terms, too. The book clearing was part of that, not leaving a mess behind him.

'And the moving around of the clocks,' Toula continued, 'was him taking control, having his independence. He arranged years ago that when he died, his business partners would come down from Athens to buy up all the clocks at a price that was good for the partner and good for me. His last effort was to arrange them in price categories and give each group a total value to keep things simple, he said. That was him just trying to maintain some control, some independence even from the grave, I think.'

Niki looked around the room. She had not noticed that the clocks had gone. The silence they left was filled with the sounds from the street coming through the open windows and shutters.

'He came down from Athens this morning,' Toula said. 'Came in a van and took the lot. Paid me money through the bank. Enough money to pay off my daughter's London mortgage, can you believe? Which I will do next week.' She sighed and began to eat her tiny sandwich in even tinier mouthfuls.

'Okay, let's go back to the hotel and sleep. I think I need to. I will wait outside. You go and tell your brother we need to leave.' Niki makes a decision to torture herself no longer by watching Petros and the girl moving ever closer together, and instead, she releases Spiros from under her resting head and walks straight back out of the canteen, out of the entrance hall, and into the atypical English sun.

There is a nip in the air though. The weather is changing.

Chapter 29

They wake late the following day but Niki insists on taking the bus, which seems to stop every few minutes to pick someone up or drop them off. Just as they come up to the long straight road that goes all the way to Canonbury and Niki is about to relax, the bus turns onto a tiny road and they spend the next twenty minutes trawling around an estate where every house is the same as the next and all of them have big grey bins outside that are full to overflowing and rubbish littered across the pavement. Niki wonders why the women do not come out and tidy up their part of the road. Do they have no pride in where they live?

Looking at her watch, she realises that she has made a bad decision. She is going to be late for her appointment at the estate agent's.

'You alright, Mama?' Spiros asks.

'Yes, it is nothing,' Niki returns. Surely they will understand if she is not there exactly at the appointed time. How many times in Greece has she been late by half an hour, sometimes a whole hour, and found that the other party is even later? It never really made a difference. Sure, the English have a reputation for being terribly precise about time, but these are just jokes, are they not? Anyway, there is nothing she can do about it now but sit and wait.

Petros is sitting behind them. He has hardly spoken to her since the incident in the main hall yesterday.

The bus finally drops them in town. The driver is kind enough to point the direction they must take and after several wrong turns and directions from helpful passersby, and another twenty minutes, they find the right place.

'Ah, Mrs...?' The man comes around from his desk and greets her with a handshake.

'Please call me Niki.' She shakes his hand warmly.

Her smile of anticipation, of hope, and her boys' good spirits are crushed within minutes. It is explained to her, with no softness, that all the flats that she has lined up to view, all the ones on the email they sent, have already been let.

'But we have appointments to see them. Here, it says so in your email.' Niki holds up the appropriate sheet and points. 'Why else would I print to all these?' She waves them under his nose.

'Twenty thousand students attend here,' the man says, but this is in no way offered as an apology. 'Most people have sorted out their accommodation by now.' Fleeting eye contact suggests his condemnation for her lax attitude. The rushing of blood twitches her legs, ready to run, but her feet do not move. Instead, her racing blood curls her fingers into fists, ready to fight.

The condemnatory look on the estate agent's face turns into fear and then settles for being guarded. Phone calls are made, alternatives are found and the man offers them a tour of the properties they have remaining.

'Of course, the quality will not be the same this late in the day,' he says, leading them out to his shiny Mini Cooper.

By the fifth flat, Niki thinks that if she has to look at one more hovel with magnolia crinkly woodchip-paper on the walls, industrial grey carpets on the floors, and a smell of damp, she might scream. If she hears this estate agent regurgitate one more banal description of what she should really be seeing as opposed to what is actually there, she might just walk out and keep walking. The first one Petros says he couldn't live in, as its filthy bathroom is shared with another flat on the same floor. Niki wanted to go out and buy some bleach and set about the place the moment she saw it.

'It will be okay. It just needs a clean,' she began, but Petros pulled her away.

The second one, a little cheaper, was not on a bus route and was too far to walk to the university, and the third was not big enough to put in a second bed. The fourth was more money, so they continued to the fifth, which is a little bigger but turns out to be the same price as the fourth. Spiros prefers the fourth, Petros the fifth. Niki doesn't like the price of either.

'The last two you have seen might be a bit more expensive, but for such sunny vistas and casual elegance, it is not overpriced. And don't forget: bills are included.' Niki makes a quick mental calculation.

'Okay, okay. We take four or five,' she says, trying to hide her impatience. It is more the attitude of the man that is exasperating her than the situation. Calling a pokey room spacious and sunlit does not make it so.

'We go now? Back to the office, make terms?' Niki demands. The estate agent agrees with a half-smile and they all climb back into his car. Spiros and Petros hunch up in the back.

As the car crawls through the walled city, the history of the place oozes through every ancient building, every stone gateway, each weathered church. They will sign a contract and this will be the boys' home in less than an hour! Niki can feel all the knots she didn't even know were there unwinding and loosening around her shoulders. After signing the contract, if they take a taxi, they can sign up for their courses and life will be perfect.

The sun comes from behind a cloud and she lets her head rest against the car window. Her neck feels soft and for the first time in days, a dull headache she hadn't even really noticed begins to lift. She wonders if she can change her ticket to return to Greece sooner. She is missing Karolos.

'So you take the fourth and fifth one?' the man says, taking off his jacket and carefully arranging it on the back of his chair.

'Which one, boys?' Niki recognises that it is not her but her boys who will be living there. It is better if it is their choice.

'Four.'

'Five.'

'Okay, I think five has more room to put a second bed.' Niki offers her advice.

'You want to put both boys into just one flat?' the man says, sounding horrified. Why does he make that sound like a problem? Her hand is on her neck, rubbing at the tension that has suddenly appeared.

Niki says slowly, cautiously, 'The boys have shared all their lives. Why not?'

'Oh, okay. But I don't really see…' The man loses his horror and his fake cheerfulness returns. 'Okay, if that's what you want. So, four or five?'

'Five.' They are agreed.

'Right, so the rent for that is...' He punches buttons on a calculator, picks up his pen, and announces brightly, 'Times two. There! That is every four weeks, not per calendar month.' He turns the calculator so Niki can see and looks over the contract, looking for the space between words where the costs needs adding and he carefully prints in the numbers.

'What do you mean "times two"?' Niki asks. The tension in her neck is somehow making her stomach turn. It might be hunger; again they have not eaten since breakfast, but she does not crave food.

'Well, the price is per person, and you want two people in the flat.' He points with the end of his pen to Spiros and then Petros. 'Then the rent is times two.'

'But *yiati* times two? One person, two people, what difference *einai*, we rent the flat?' Niki can hear her Greek getting mixed up with her English but it all rushes out of her at such a speed, she has no control.

'Ah, no, you see two people means two lots of wear and tear. Also, the landlord has to find another bed.'

'I will buy a bed.' All her tension is back.

'I' m afraid...' The man begins.

'The same for flat four?' Niki asks. He nods, his mouth somewhere between a smile and a smirk. She would like to slap him.

'Wait,' Niki says, holding the flat of her hand in his face. *Mountza*! That feels good. It may not be an offensive action in this country but for her, she knows, she has just cursed him.

He is silent. Niki uses the time to do some mental calculations.

'Okay,' she says with authority. 'You take half for the second boy.'

The man gasps, then frowns and exhales as if he cannot believe her words.

'You take or we go.' Niki presses her point. Her stomach is turning over, her palms are sweaty.

'I can make a call,' he offers weakly and picks up the phone. They sit in silence as the phone connects, and then there is much jolly laughing from the man as he talks very quickly into the phone.

When the conversation finishes, he sits back with authority.

'He says you can take number four for one and a half times the price.' His elbows on the armrests, his fingers steepled as he leans back in his chair.

'Done.' Niki does not wait for more. She has done the maths. Bills are included, and she never expected that, so overall, it works out as a better price. At last, something is going in her favour.

'Great!' His eyes light up. He takes out a new contract and writes the newly calculated figures where spaces have been left.

'So we need a deposit of...' He taps the monthly rent into his calculator. 'Times twelve.' He taps again.

'What? Why twelve?' Niki's stomach collapses.

'Are you British citizens?' The pen hovers.

'We are EU.' Niki sits up straight. Spiros copies her. Petros is watching the girl at the back of the office who is typing. She glances up and smiles at him.

'Ah, yes the EU, which is not the UK. If you do not live in the UK, then we need the first year up front.'

'What?' Niki's mouth is dry and her tongue adheres to the roof of her mouth.

'Too many foreign students coming and moving in and then either leaving suddenly or not paying the rent.'

'But we will pay.' Niki unsticks her tongue.

'It is the rule.'

'Call him again, this Mr. Landlord. Call him and tell him we are not these people who do not pay.'

'Sorry.' He sits back, fingers interlocked across his chest this time.

'I go somewhere else.' Niki puts her hands on the arms of the chair as if to stand.

'I think you will find it is the same everywhere,' he says, almost kindly. 'Too many have been burnt.'

'Burnt? What has fire got to do with this?' She can feel herself shaking now. She is not sure if it is anger or if she is about to collapse, cry, curl into a ball and never take part on life again.

'No, burnt, as in losing money.'

'But this is not me.' Her voice sounds quiet, without authority.

'I understand.' He unlocks his fingers and leans over the desk toward her. 'But it is the rules.'

'Come boys, we go. This man is a crook.' Niki stands, a tall son either side of her.

'Go!' The man also stands. 'You will find it is the same everywhere you go,' he calls after them as the bell on the door rings behind them.

Chapter 30

The estate agency two doors down has two rows of desks, but only one person at any of them, and there are no lights on even though the day is becoming duller and duller. The girl, who is not much older than Petros and Spiros, assures Niki, with much sympathy, that it is the same all over town. Foreigners must pay a year's rent in advance.

'But how do they expect us to do this? How can someone who wants better for their children but is not rich manage, and then they want the fees all together. It is so inhuman. How...' But Niki has run out of words and energy.

'Oh you poor thing.' The girl sounds genuine. 'You're Greek, right?' she enquires. 'Well, here's what I would do.' She stresses the word *I*. 'The Greeks round here are a close-knit community, so go up to Yamas, on the next street. George runs it, nice bloke. Greek. He has so many cousins and what-have-you. Ask him if he knows of anywhere your boys can stay until they find their feet.' She looks from Niki to Spiros and then her eyes linger on Petros. He returns her smiles and subtly tenses his folded arms so his biceps show.

Niki glances at her own feet. She has found them, but she realises this is not what the girl means. It must be a saying. However, she is too tired to ask the meaning.

'Come on.' Petros is still grinning and flexing and Niki nudges him harshly in the ribs. This is no time for his flirting ways. Why do the boys not do anything to make this dream happen? All the energy is hers; what have they done? Nothing, that's what. They sit back and let her do it all, just like their baba. The only time Petros shows any interest in anything is when a girl gives him some attention.

Niki is out of the door without even a *thank you* to the girl behind the desk.

Yamas has an ageing, brightly coloured plastic sign above the window. The whole place looks like it has seen better days. Someone has written the menu with a white pen on the inside of the window, and much of it has smudged near the tables that are up against the glass. The words *All Day Breakfast* are scrawled in capitals.

'Oh yes, I'm starving.' Petros is first through the door; Niki and Spiros follow. She wants coffee. Greek coffee. A pita bread would be nice, with a few chips and slices of fresh tomato, satisfying and comforting.

'Yamas.' A big, smiling man with a mass of black hair and dark eyes welcomes them from behind his stainless steel counter, spatula in hand, a dirty apron around his waist. A thin woman flashes them a look and continues to spoon hot fat over a sizzling egg in a grime-encrusted pan.

'Yeia sas. Ti kanete? Ellinikos kafes yparxei?'

The man stares back at her, his smile frozen.

'*Kafes*?' Niki asks again, but the sinking in her stomach convinces her that there is more of this terrible day to come.

'You know, I have lost nearly all my Greek now, but they still call me George the Greek.' The man finds his own words amusing. 'Been here forty years now. All day, nothing but English. You forget.' His grin is even wider. 'You are going to the university?' he addresses the boys.

'Yes,' Spiros answers.

'I got my degree there. Such fun days. You have a good mother, boys. She is wanting the best for you.'

Niki reassess him. Over the grill, a sign says *The Chef is Always Right*. A piece of cardboard folded over so it stands on top of the cash till reads *No credit* with three exclamation marks in black marker pen and in red biro underneath, it says, *This means you!!*

'What degree did you take?' Niki asks bluntly.

'Ah ha! Business. Had this big plan that I was going back to Greece, work in a hotel for some experience, build my own hotel on my baba's land ...' He trails off but soon resumes his narrative. 'But the lease came up on this, and I had worked here whilst I studied. It seemed like a perfect way of learning what universities cannot teach you. And here I am. Now, what can I get you?' He grins throughout his speech.

The woman pours the egg and its grease from the frying pan onto a waiting buttered slice of bread and then, quite unexpectedly, she calls, 'Table six,' in a shrill, harsh, high-pitched tone.

A man near the window puts down his paper and his mug of coffee and collects his plate, taking a bottle of ketchup from the counter with him.

Niki notes a carved wooden donkey, with rush baskets on either side of its red blanket saddle, sitting on top of the cash register, the pictures of Mykonos, Zakinthos, and Santorini on the walls. Two round-bottomed, straw-covered bottles make an attempt at decoration on a shelf by a door marked *Toilet*. It is lifeless and dull and Niki wonders how the man can live like this. There is none of the vibrancy of Stella's eatery. There is no banter between customers, no central drinks cabinet that you can help yourself from and let Stella know what you have taken when you pay, something which gives her place such a personal feel. Niki's chest fills with yearning. She would like to be back there right now, with the sun streaming down, dogs sniffing on the square, men arguing in the *kafeneio*, a simple life that they can afford with ease. Is all this pushing to get her boys a better life that they cannot afford really any better?

Out the window, even the sun is hiding behind a cloud which seems to be spreading and covering the whole sky in one flat sheet.

'All day breakfast,' Petros answers George the Greek's question. English breakfast is his latest favourite, Niki has noticed. Maybe he does not hunger after blue skies and friendly banter.

'Same here,' Spiros agrees enthusiastically.

'I don't suppose you do Greek coffee, do you?' Niki asks, the hope in her voice evident.

'Sorry, no. Can do you a frappe.' George seems to find everything he says funny.

Niki wants to say, 'Frappe? In this weather?' but bites her tongue.

'No, hot coffee, and a toast.' Then she remembers that toast in this county means grilled bread. 'I mean cheese and ham in bread that is toasted,' she explains.

'Can we do that, Stef?' He turns to the woman, who nods but does not take her eyes off the chips she is shaking over the fryer.

The Formica table is chipped round the edges. Niki cups her mug with her hands and looks first at Spiros and then Petros.

'You want this, boys?' As she says the words, she realises it is the first time she has ever asked them.

'What, Mama?' Spiros asks, the tone sounding like his baba.

'You want this?' she repeats and indicates with her thumb the café and then the grey outside, where it has now started to rain, the cars on the road hissing as they kick up wet from the puddles that are quickly forming.

'I don't understand,' Spiros says.

'If you say it is good, we believe you, Mama,' Petros says. Niki reaches across the table and takes his hand. He is a good boy. A flirt, but a good boy.

'But do you want it?' Niki implores them, her free hand reaching for Spiros, holding both their hands across the table, looking them in the eyes.

Neither of them speaks.

'We are running around like chickens in a coop and every which way we turn, there is a wall so high, we cannot get over. They say Greece is in the EU and make promises of all that is possible. They do not add that it is possible only for the rich. Who do we know who has gone to a foreign university? No one. Why? Is it because they don't want to? No! Because they cannot afford it.'

'Themis went,' Petros offers.

'Themis went back to Athens when he was fifteen to finish his education at a fee-paying school. His uncle is a politician; his family is rich. That is what I am saying. It is only for the rich. I have been trying to reach a dream that is maybe not for poor farmers like us. It was just a carrot that they hang before us as if we are donkeys, there to tempt us into believing the Euro was a good idea and that the Drachma was a relic of the past. But really, they steal from us. They steal our identity, they tempt us with plastic cards that get you in debt, and ambition that we cannot attain, and when it all goes wrong, then they blame us!' Niki tries to keep her voice quiet but she cannot stop the tears flowing.

Her boys take their hands out from under hers and put them on top, holding her fingers. Spiros strokes her forearm with his other hand. They wait for her to gain control.

'I am sorry, boys. I think I have misled you. You worked so hard. Spiros, I am so proud of you for coming top in all the school, and there is no doubt you deserve this dream. Petros, you have been so patient waiting a year, doing nothing, until your brother catches up with you so we could do all this.' She rolls her eyes over all that she can see. 'Together. But...'

'Number eight. Two full English.' The harsh, high-pitched screech makes them all jump.

'That is us, Mama,' Spiros says gently as he releases her hand and jumps up to get the tray.

They eat in silence. She wants to tell Petros not to use so much ketchup. It is bright red! It is not Stella's home-made sauce, and he has no idea what might be in it, but she cannot find her voice—or any enthusiasm.

'So how you find your breakfast?' George with his mass of black hair comes over to make sure everything is alright.

'Good,' Petros says enthusiastically.

'Your cheese and ham toastie okay, Madam?'

'Yes, yes. Thank you,' Niki answers. He seems a kind man, but she can't help thinking he would be happier back in Greece. Maybe he has some pride in his café, but it does not show. It might be kind of her to tell him that he has been recommended. 'The estate agent down the road suggested we came here.'

'Who, Zoe? Good girl, Zoe. She used to work here but they offered her more money.'

'I don't know her name. She also said you might know someone who can put up my boys. We cannot find anywhere for them to stay.' Niki says this with no energy and very little interest. It seems such a long shot.

'Well, I do have a cousin with houses. I can call him and ask if you like.'

'Yes please.' Niki does not allow herself to feel any hope.

'If you boys stay, I need two workers. You want extra work whilst you study?' The man looks at Petros and Spiros. They are both still eating, but both nod. 'I need someone to cook.' He looks back at the woman, who has her back to him where she tends the stove. 'Stefi is going back to Cyprus at the end of the week. And I need someone to serve, take Zoe's place. With you being brothers, it adds a nice touch. Greek brothers, yes!' He slaps his hands together and rubs them on each other as if trying to warm them, but it is not cold in the café. The windows are steamed up with the rain outside.

'So, I will call my cousin.' And away he bustles.

An hour later, after extra toast and marmalade for Petros and a second coffee for Niki, the cousin turns up in a rusting Mercedes. George the Greek waves them off as he puts their payment in the till.

The cousin looks very much like George, only he does not have a mass of black hair. Instead, there is a ring of grey, and he is bald on top. His gold cufflinks dangle as he drives.

'So, you come from the Greece,' he says, his accent thick.

'*Nai*,' Niki answers and they strike up a conversation in Greek about how the people are coping and how hard it is in Greece, and how the West tempts them but then denies them and although the conversation expands on everything Niki has been feeling, it only succeeds in depressing her. She cannot be bothered to keep her face animated and she can almost feel her cheeks sagging. She knows she is beginning to look old, but right now, she does not care.

The flat they are shown is miles from the university, but George's cousin assures her that the bus is on a direct route and points out the bus stop before they go inside.

It smells of damp and fried food. The carpet in the hall is so ingrained with dirt, it is impossible to make out the colour or even if it ever had a pattern.

The room he offers them is the first on the left. It is a plain room with a bay window and a double bed that takes up most of the space. The bed is visibly sunken in the middle and the walls need a fresh coat of paint. Someone comes through the front door and pounds up the stairs, then a door bangs and music soaks through the ceiling.

The shared kitchen is filthy, the toilet has water constantly running down a brown stain in the pan, the shower door is missing, and there is black mould growing between all the wall tiles.

'How much?' Niki asks. Petros has a look of horror on his face as she says this. Spiros is staying close to her.

The amount he wants is less than the last place and 'Yes,' he assures them, 'bills are included.'

'Okay, we take it,' Niki says.

Petro's look of horror becomes more apparent and Spiros mutters 'Mama?' very quietly in her ear.

'Boys, we cannot be choosers. We came here with an idea that we would not take a place with a shared bathroom or kitchen, or a place near a noisy road, or nowhere too far from the university or this or that, but the truth is we do not have a choice. We must take what is offered. Next year, because we now know how it all works, we will be ready.'

'You want it?' The man asks without much interest but with a hint of surprise.

'Yes,' Niki affirms.

'Okay, so I need a year up front and a month's deposit.' He is examining the banister rail that has come loose.

'We cannot do that,' Niki says. 'We pay two months' rent and a month deposit. That is all we can afford.' She is not aggressive, nor is she authoritative, she is just honest.

His head shines in the unshaded bulb as he looks at his watch.

'Sorry, no can do,' he says, inspecting his gold watch. He drums his fingers on the banister.

'Then I am sorry.' Niki heads for the door, her boys following. Once they are all outside, she adds,

'Is there nothing we can do?' The way she finds herself looking at him catapults her back to her first days in Greece, her need for a bed, and what she had to do to get it.

'I have another appointment.' The man does not even answer her. 'You can find your own way back, okay?' But it is not a question. Then he is in the car and gone, leaving them standing in the drizzle.

Chapter 31

They wait, uncertain what to do next and getting wetter by the minute. Four buses have passed, none of them in the right direction until, 'Mama there is a bus.'

Spiros points to a bus that has *University* written on the window above the driver, and they flag it down. It stops a few meters up the road and they run in response to the revving engine.

Apart from the windscreen, the bus windows are blanked out with condensation and people sit, looking uncomfortable in plastic coats, umbrellas wetting their legs. The lights are on in the bus, giving everything a faint orange glow. It is not an unfriendly atmosphere.

Spiros insists Niki take a seat while he buys tickets from the driver. Niki finds a double seat for her boys and sits in front of them next to a man who smiles. He is a little older than her boys and he does not look English.

'Hello. How are you?' he opens.

It feels like the first piece of unsolicited kindness she has received since leaving Greece.

'Hello.' She is too tired to say any more.

'You go to the university?'

'No. My sons, they try to go.' Then she realises he probably means is she going to the university now, on the bus, but she does not correct herself.

'How you mean they try?' he says. Niki cannot place his accent.

'The university wants them but the flats want a year's money to live there. I have money, but not that much money.' Her chest rises as she takes a big breath and then releases what tension she can.

'Ah yes,' the man says and then remains silent for a minute or two. The hissing of the rain under the tyres is audible where they are sitting over the wheel arch. The girl in front has on headphones, and Niki can hear the beat and almost make out the melody. Her instinct is to tell the girl to turn the volume down, that she will damage her ears.

Behind her, Petros has his eyes closed. Spiros looks exhausted and sad.

'I have the same problem,' the man says.

Niki looks at him. He has an unusual profile. His forehead slopes back quite steeply above his eyebrows and his nose is almost flat. His lower lip is full but his upper lip is almost absent.

'Yes, I get a grant, and a scholarship, so I have no fees to pay and I have money for a flat, but I am trying to find one I like.'

'Everywhere except the worse places are taken,' Niki informs him.

'I like to have space, so I have been looking for a two bedroom place. Those do not go so quickly. I have seen a good one near the university. I just need for a paper to come through from my uncle and then it is mine if I want it.'

'You are very lucky and I wish you well.'

'Yes, indeed I am lucky. But you say your boys have been offered a place at the university?'

'Yes, that is all done. They studied so hard.' This fills her with sadness and she blinks a couple of times to stop any tears from forming.

'It is criminal that for the want of somewhere to stay, they do not go. They have done the hard work.'

'Yes, I agree.'

'So what do you do now?' he asks.

'I don't know. I suppose I go back to the university, see if they have any cancellations for the halls of residency.'

'And if not?'

Niki has been trying to avoid this thought. She knows the answer: they will return to Greece, the boys' places will be deferred, and then she will have the same nightmare next year, but with a little more knowledge. If she carries on at the water board, hopefully there will be a little more money, but there are no guarantees. She needs thousands, not the few hundred she has diverted to help her boys. For that, Karolos will have to be paid for the oranges he sold the year before last, and next year's oranges.

Her headache bites harder. It may only have been a few hundred that she diverted from other peoples' accounts to her own, and it may well not be noticed. Also, it may be for a good cause but now she is here in the home country of those foreigners, it eats at her that she has taken what is not hers.

England is not a place where the streets are paved with gold, no matter what they say. The

English people who buy houses in Greece have made a living here in a land where nothing seems human, where everything has a rule and a regulation, where all is decided by these pre-set recommendations and no one seems to talk of individual needs. These English, she decides, have earned their money the hard way. If she had been brought up here, she too would want to move, to escape the inhuman rules and regulations.

It makes a mockery of why she wants to send her sons here.

'Everything has two sides,' she says under her breath. Take away the humanity of Greece and replace it with rules, and it would be like England and lose its heart. Take the rules out of England and replace it with heart, and it would decline like Greece. There is no winning situation.

She looks out into the grey day, the rain making the tarmac and buildings shiny. Even in the wet, the old buildings are so beautiful, they are hard to believe. How wonderful to live in such a place and see them every day. But then to actually make a living here when everyone is so insular and unfriendly? It would pull out her soul and leave nothing but an empty shell. Maybe that is why she has seen so many blank faces and empty smiles. Why no one on the bus is chatting to anyone they don't know.

How many times has she made a new friend on the bus to Saros? So often that they are now all old friends. There is no division in Greece between work and play, not in the village or Saros anyway. You chat, you have coffee, you talk to your friends on the phone and it all gets mixed up with the papers you need to order and numbers you need to put in the computer, or in Karolos' case, the oranges he needs to dust with pesticide, the stones he must clear off the land. All is play and life is work. All is work and life is play.

'I have an idea.' The man next to her wakes her from her thoughts. 'If I can get this paper from my uncle and I can get this place, then why do your boys not live in the other room I will have? They can pay rent, but I would not ask for a year's rent up front, nor double. I would ask for nothing but a month's rent. Yes, why not? They have done the work, and they deserve their places.'

Niki can only stare at him. Spiros leans forward to listen to their conversation.

'Frank.' He holds out his hand for her to shake. It is slightly clammy but the grip is firm.

'Niki. Are you serious?' she says, trying to calm her heart that has decided to beat with hope even though her head tells her nothing has happened yet.

'I am absolutely serious,' Frank says. She looks from one of his eyes to the other, trying to gauge his sincerity. The whites are more yellow than white and his eyes are such a dark brown, she cannot see where the iris ends and his pupils start. 'We are going up to the university stop now. Give me your phone number and I will see what I can do and I will call you tomorrow.'

'I do not have phone, but here,' she fiddles in her pocket. 'This is where I am staying. Room 17.' She hands him the hotel's business card. 'Call me. Please. My boys' future depends on you.' She cannot help herself: her hope has returned and with it, her energy.

They leave Frank where he is sitting and wave as the bus pulls away. When it turns the corner, Niki does a little dance on the wet pavement.

'Maybe the gods are smiling on us, boys. Maybe the universe would not bring us so far in our journey without making a way possible.' The boys' moods lift with her energy and the three of them practically dance into the university building.

The woman in charge of such things confirms that no places in halls have become free and as she looks through her records and takes their names, she points out that they have not even registered their interest, so a place could not be offered them anyway. Niki remembers that she was interrupted by running to stop the boys for registering.

'Can I register now?' she asks.

The woman says she can but kindly informs her that there is very little hope.

The taxi they call turns out to be Brian again, and he is very pleased to see them and recounts a jolly tale about his granddaughter's third birthday party yesterday. Something about a game the children were playing and how he was left in a cupboard for an hour, but his English is too fast and

Niki feels too tired, and strangely excited, to concentrate.

Back in the hotel room, she and her boys flop onto the beds and kick their shoes off.

'I think it is going to happen,' Niki says. 'I really do. I feel hopeful about Frank.'

'But Mama, he was just a man in the bus.' Spiros' negative voice sounds like Karolos.

'But he has a flat, he has spare rooms. And why not, Spiros? Why should we not have some luck? Why should this Frank not be the person who answers our dreams?'

Spiros stays silent.

They all lay looking up at the ceiling.

After half an hour, she can hear Spiros' rhythmical breathing.

'I'm hungry,' Petros says.

Niki thinks for a moment. Her feet are sore from walking; she is generally tired from the last two days. If Frank does not want anything up front over the first month's rent, then they have money to spare.

Rolling over to the bedside table, she picks up the menu and throws it at Petros.

'Here,' she says, sounding and feeling a little naughty, a touch decadent. 'Let's order room service.'

Chapter 32

Niki dreams of Toula. It is part dream, part recollection of their conversation. The shutters are all open but the room is in semi-darkness. The clock pendulums swing, glinting in and out of the light of the table lamps, but there is no ticking. Toula is eating a sandwich, sharing it with a bird that perches on the edge of her plate.

'We are in a dream now,' she says to the bird.

'Yes we are,' the bird replies.

'So we can say what we like and no one will ever know.' Toula addresses Niki, who has three uneaten sandwiches on her plate. She cannot eat, as her mouth is dry and there is no tea in her cup.

'You knew he was stuck in the lift. You left him to die.' Niki only thinks this, but in the dream Toula hears her thoughts.

'At what point are you dead? When the heart stops beating or when you stop living?' Toula asks.

She pours the tea.

'They are the same,' Niki replies.

'Are they? When I was in London, I tried to cross a road to see Buckingham Palace. As you know, I am old and I do not walk so fast. But a taxi came with so much speed that I ran. Yes me, I ran. I found life in my limbs I did not know I had, and when I got to the other side, everything was different. Colours seemed brighter, sounds clearer. People came up to me to see if I was alright. Their kindness crept into the very centre of my heart and I felt loved by strangers. I felt more alive than I had done in years and it was all because I came close to death.'

The tea keeps pouring but the cup does not fill. There is only one sandwich on the floral patterned plate on Niki's knee now although she has eaten nothing.

'Are you saying your husband felt more alive in that last week because you left him to die?' the bird asks.

'Did I? I don't remember that,' Toula says.

'What are you saying?' Niki asks. The plate of sandwiches on her knee has been replaced by the stolen book. She tries to hide it with her napkin.

'Are there such things as accidents, or do we bring about what we need to happen to us?'

Niki realises that until this point, they have been speaking English.

'It was Apostolis' selfishness that made him unhappy. It meant he was always looking inward and therefore only saw himself. It was this that made him unhappy and made my life miserable too. Not fixing the lift appears to have nothing to do with his inward looking. But I ask you, would the internal change that Apostolis would have had to have made to become the person who would have fixed the lift also be the change that he would have had to have made to become a happy, loving, kind man? To find the motivation to fix the lift, he would have had to think how it was for me and for you using it. Often, the very shift we need to fix ourselves is the shift we are unprepared to make and so we keep going around in circles.'

'Circles,' the bird repeats. 'Like being stuck in a lift again and again.'

'So when we make an accident happen, is that our subconscious trying to make us do something differently? Forcing us to change so we can become whole? Nearly being run over by a taxi could have been avoided if I was a little more patient and looked both ways. But nearly being hit opened my eyes and my heart and made life so much more precious. Maybe my subconscious made that accident happen so I would realise that there is not time to wait to see my daughter and grandchildren. The time is now. There is no other time.'

'Not a reply,' the bird squawks.

'I'm sorry, I did not hear you my little friend. Age does many things to a body, but one thing most of us can be sure of is a little deafness,' Toula says to the bird.

'Simply die,' the bird squawks and flies out the window.

'You've been a good friend to me over the years.' The old lady ignores the empty space the bird has left and addresses Niki, who looks down to her knee, where the book has turned into a key.

'And you have been kind to me,' Niki replies, wondering if the key is stolen like the book was. Does she need to hide it?

'Speak up, dear,' Toula says and her arms start to sprout feathers.

There is no reason to awake sweating from this dream, but Niki does. It felt like an answer but with sinister undertones. Before she slept, she could have told you what had really been said, but now she cannot remember which is dream and which is reality.

Something tells her that Toula might not have heard Apostolis cry for help. But how else would she know the sound she heard that day when she stood with the key in the lock was the noise like a cat whining? What did the bird say in the dream? 'Like being stuck in a lift again and again.' Maybe the last time was not the first time Apostolis was stuck in the lift? Maybe Toula knew it was a whine from times before? But if she knew it was possible for him to be stuck in the lift, would she really leave him for two weeks when there was a chance he might use it?

She puts her hands to her head, the words going round and round. 'Circles,' the bird said. Well, that is how it feels. In their real conversation the day she visited Toula, the old lady went round in circles, telling her again and again what a good friend she had been, how she would not have been able to bear her life over the last years if it had not been for Niki's twice-weekly visits. How it had kept her sane and given her something to look forward to.

'The young think life is all about chasing a little comfort, a little luxury. They are right. But they think it is the comfort and luxury that money can buy, like a shiny car, a nice dress. They are wrong,' Toula said.

'The only truly valuable thing on this earth is the comfort of another person. How can I repay that luxury?'

Niki lets these thoughts drift. The daylight is peeking between the curtains, and sleep has gone for the night. She still has the headache left over from yesterday and now there is a layer of grogginess on top, the dream becoming more real than the true events, the reality fading.

Maybe she will never know if Toula heard her husband, if he cried out and she ignored him. Nor can she be sure that she heard him, either. Maybe it really was a cat. The rumours suggested there was a cat in the lift with him when they found him and the gossip mongers added with relish that the cat had not starved. Niki does not like to dwell on this imagery.

The shower is as hot as she can bear. The dream still lingers. The only way to get it out of her mind will be to talk to someone, take that leap into being fully awake. Slipping on her clothes, she goes out to reception. It is still early but Frank just might have called.

The girl there looks tired. It is the end of her shift. She confirms that there have been no calls. An equally tired-looking new girl arrives, yawns, and takes the first girl's seat.

'Morning,' she says to Niki, putting her hand over her mouth as she yawns again.

'I am expecting a call,' Niki tells her. 'Is it possible to put it through to my room, Number 17, when it comes? Can that be something that can happen?'

'Sure,' the girl replies.

Padding back to her room, her sense of loneliness makes her wonder if she should not call Karolos. It might be good for the boys to hear his voice, too.

Chapter 33

'Hello, Karolos?'

'Hello, Niki, why you call? You alright? The boys okay? Where are you?'

'England.'

'Oh! How does it go? You sound so close.'

'Let me talk to him, Mama.' Petros makes a grab for the phone. 'Hey Baba. You must come to England. It is full of life—and girls.'

Spiros pulls the mouthpiece away from him. 'It is wet, Baba, and the sky is grey, and there is nowhere to stay.'

'What? What do you mean, nowhere to stay?'

Niki takes back the receiver.

'There is a problem with the rooms. The university have none and everywhere else says that the boys must pay each, they cannot share, and they want a year's rent up front.'

'You are speaking nonsense, Niki. I have been learning the laptop, I have looked, there are many many rooms in that town. They do not say they will charge for a year or extra for another boy.'

'They tell you when you go and see them.'

'No, Niki *mou*, you are wrong. Look, here is one, one bedroom, own bathroom, fifteen minutes' walk from the university ..."

Niki closes her eyes. Why is he learning to use the Internet now when all that preparatory work has already been done? He is too late to be useful.

'Karolos, I have been into estate agents here. It is all the same: we must pay, and pay and pay,' Niki explains.

'Here is a private one, no estate agent, one bedroom, own bathroom...'

'I have also gone to a private landlord, a Greek, and he also wanted a year up front.'

'A Greek? Did you tell him you were Greek?'

'We spoke Greek together.'

'You explained?"

'Of course.'

'And he did not make it possible?'

'No.' Niki tries to remain patient. Her grip tightens on the receiver.

'Then he was not Greek!' Karolos explodes. 'Go back to the estate agent, Niki. I will tell you which ones and what they have on offer. Maybe you should get them to call me. I will explain.'

'You think we have not tried?' Her eyes sting; she blinks back the tears.

'Baba.' Spiros leans towards the mouthpiece. 'What Mama says is right. We have tried.' Even young Spiros sounds beaten. Niki feels a little frown pass over her brow. Maybe the disappointment of all this is too much for him. He has never been as resilient as Petros. She will watch him carefully.

'Niki? What will you do now? Do you give up?' It is hard to tell whether Karolos sounds relieved or disappointed.

'I met a boy. Well, a man, called Frank on the bus yesterday. He says he is getting a flat today with a spare room the boys can have for the price of one, no year up front.' As Niki says this her eyes close, her cheeks rise, her nose crinkles. Something feels not quite right about Frank.

'Ah, there you are, you see. I told you! You use a private landlord, no agents, and they are willing to let two stay in one room. It is only logical with them being brothers.'

'Well, he said he would ring if he gets the room. He needed a paper from his uncle or something.'

'So when does he ring?'

'I don't know. Maybe he doesn't. Maybe it was all too good to be true.'

'And you accuse me of not being optimistic. Niki *mou*, this man, it seems, has offered you a gift. Trust it will happen. Why would this man say he had a room and that the boys could have it if he didn't have a room and the boys could not have it?'

'Yes,' is all Niki can think to answer. He doesn't understand. The rules are different here. Everything is more complicated and nothing is as it seems. People do not work together in the way they do back in Greece. It is not an easy place to be.

'So you call me again when it is all arranged.' Karolos is full of energy.

'Okay.' She passes the receiver to the boys and lies down. The boys say their goodbyes, Petros tells Karolos about the girl in the cafeteria in the university, and Karolos says something that makes him laugh. The stress that she wasn't aware was on his young face lifts and he looks more like a boy than a man. After the phone call, the room seems very silent.

Spiros lies down. Petros sits on the floor with his back against the double bed.

The jangle of the phone ringing so soon after talking to Karolos makes them all jump.

'Hello. Niki. It is Frank.'

'It's Frank,' Niki tells the boys, her hand over the mouthpiece. 'Hello Frank.' She tries to sound more carefree than she feels. 'How is the flat? Did you get it?'

'Yes,' says Frank and Niki nods and smiles at the boys who leap up, big grins, wide eyes.

'Well, sort of,' Frank adds. Niki frowns.

'What do you mean?' The boys become still at these words, and huddle around Niki to listen.

'Well, I can get the room but my uncle he says all the papers have not come through yet. A part of the grant has come but not all. I am short by a thousand pounds.'

'Oh.' Niki slumps.

'But he says the money will be transferred tomorrow, so it is alright.'

'Oh.' Niki sits up.

'But they say the flat, because it is so close to the university, will be gone by tomorrow. It would have saved on time and bus fares, as it is just across the road. The other place I was looking at is a distance away. I will need a bus pass—that's five hundred pounds a year! But never mind, what can we do?'

Niki slumps. The boys look at her with yearning, longing, desperate hope in their faces.

'Unless...' Frank says slowly.

'Unless what?' Niki replies with caution.

'Well, if you could lend me the thousand just for today, I could sign the lease this afternoon. We could move in this evening.'

Niki holds the receiver against her chest.

'He wants me to lend him a thousand pounds to get the flat today. He will pay us back tomorrow.'

Spiros shrugs, the corners of his mouth curling down, his chin jutting forward.

Petros shakes his head. '*Oxi* Mama, I do not trust him.' He does not speak boldly, his voice unsure.

'But this is our last chance. He will pay me back tomorrow,' Niki implores.

'Niki? Niki, are you there?' Frank can be heard by them all.

'Yes, I am here, Frank. A thousand pounds is a lot of money. I am very interested but I just need to explain it to my sons. Can you call back in five minutes? Is it okay? We will not lose the flat if you call back in five minutes?'

'Oh.' He sounds surprised. 'Well, if you need to talk. But I think the longer we leave it, the more chance we have that we will lose it.'

'Okay Frank. Five minutes total. Yes?'

'Okay.' And the line goes dead.

'He could be a con man, Mama,' Petros says.

'I do not think so. He seems so genuine. He might just be a very kind man who is like us, in a bit of a muddle over everything,' Spiros says.

'It might be our only chance,' Niki reminds them.

But she has not hung up on Frank to explain to the boys. Lifting her shirt, she undoes the money belt and takes out the handful of cash. She is not sure she has enough left to pay the thousand pounds and still cover the university fees and for whatever else the new flat needs. Everything has cost so much. She has spent what feels like a small fortune on taxis, buses, food, and the hotel already. So much has gone so quickly.

She counts, does sums in her head. To give up a thousand pounds will leave them very short. She will have the cash for the university fees, but she would be able to buy nothing for the flat. What if there is no second bed? What about linen?

The phone rings.

'Hello Frank. Look, I want to be honest with you. If I give you a thousand, it would leave us very short of money. I would not be able to get a second bed or...'

'Five hundred then?' Frank interrupts her.

Petros rolls his eyes and shakes his head in disbelief.

Spiros nods. 'That is a good deal, Mama. It is less than we were expecting to pay as a deposit.' Niki nods her reply to him, ignoring Petros. It is a good deal.

'Don't do it, Mama,' Petros hisses and he puts his finger on the phone lugs so it beeps and the line is once again dead.

'What did you do that for?' Niki explodes. There is no way to call Frank back, but after a minute, the phone rings again and she snatches it up.

'Frank?'

'No, Karolos. Did he call?'

'Ah, hi, yes he called but he's short of money by... Well, he said a thousand, but when I said I didn't have a thousand, he said five hundred would do. He'll pay me back tomorrow.'

'Oh, he sounds very obliging.'

'It's a lot of money with no guarantees. Should I give it to him?'

'Sure. Maybe ask him a few more questions. But why would he say he needed the money if he didn't?'

'Mama, Frank might be trying to call back.' Spiros nudges her.

'Look, I will call you, Karolos. Frank might be trying to call, okay?'

'Mama, how come the amount Frank needed went from a thousand to five hundred in the space of a second when you said you couldn't afford it?' Petros asks.

Niki and Spiros both become still.

'Well, I don't know. Maybe he had some extra but didn't want to use it. Like we didn't.' But Niki feels no more sure than she sounds. She counts out five hundred.

'Sure, why not,' Spiros agrees, looking from Petros to Niki and back.

The phone rings. Petros grabs it.

'We got cut off.' It is Frank's voice.

'Yes, this is Petros.'

There is a just the slightest hesitation.

'So, how soon can you get me the five hundred? I can be there in half an hour to pick it up. It will take me about an hour to sort out the paperwork for the room and then I can send a taxi to get you?'

Niki tries to take the phone from Petros, but he turns away from her.

'That would be great, Frank. Very kind of you to offer to send a taxi. Only we cannot manage the five hundred.' Petros takes the phone from his ear and turns to point it at Niki and Spiros so they can both hear.

'Oh, okay. Well, maybe I can arrange it with two hundred, then.' Frank's voice sounds hard and his words clipped. There is an edge of desperation.

'One hundred,' Petros says.

'One hundred? It is hardly worth...' but he does not finish his sentence.

'Worth what? The con?' Petros says.

Niki gasps and grabs for the phone, but the line is dead.

'He's gone!'

'Of course he's gone, Mama. I called his bluff. He was afraid.'

Despite her desperate need to believe the opposite, Niki knows what Petros is saying is true. Her momentary bubbling of anger towards him subsides as quickly as it arose. It is not he who is at fault. She should give him and Spiros a cuddle, but all her limbs feel heavy. In a minute. She will give them support in a minute. Her dull headache is back. If she could be anywhere right now, she would like to be cleaning Toula's main room, in the calm, undisturbed, unchanging, timeless, half-light that makes it seem like the world outside does not exist. A place where she is not under pressure to assure her boys their future, cook, or support or plan or push. A place where there is no rush and she becomes lost in the moment. No before. No after.

'Here is the difference,' Toula said. 'The days here in this room with Apostolis pass, one after the other. Tick-tick, his clocks ring out the passing of each second.' She paused to listen to the clocks, out of time with each other so there is no moment of quiet. 'Each tick turns into a minute and each minute to an hour and the hours pass and the days merge and you turn around and the years have gone by, but because of this semi-gloom, because of this unchanging room, this tomb, there is no indication that time has passed and yet years have gone and I have been able to do nothing with my life.' She paused, took a deep breath which caused her head to wobble. 'And I resent it!' Her words were loud, heartfelt.

Niki opened her mouth to speak. She was not sure what to say, but some note of sympathy seemed in order.

'And that is the difference,' Toula continued. 'When you are here, Niki my friend, you bring life and conversation, news of the village. Time flies by even faster but never with resentment, only joy in that time passing. There is no thought of having not achieved anything with my life in that time when you are here. The difference is time passes even faster but with no looking back, only forward. That, Niki my dear, is time well spent.'

It was about then that Niki wondered why Toula had asked her over. It was nice to talk and it was true to character that the old woman would want to tell her to her face that she was going to live with her daughter and that the job would no longer exist. But there was something in the way Toula was speaking that Niki could not help but feel that she had an agenda.

The time so far in England has not felt well spent. It has been all about rushing and pushing and frustration and stress. She has not dared to think about the future because she has not been able to control the present and in every second of her present, it has felt as if she has been shown up for being naïve and greedy. Frank is the perfect example of her greed and lack of control, her desperation and her naivety. The ultimate humiliation. It is easy to be honest with herself now and admit that really, all along, she sensed Frank was not as he seemed. After all, what were the chances of meeting someone on the bus who would have a flat with a spare room and it all work out perfectly? She had known. Only she had not wanted to know. Just like when she first arrived in Greece. She knew the price of her bed for the night, but she pretended to herself that it was not so, that it was something else: friendship, cuddles. At least this time, things were stopped before they had gone too far. Heat rises in her cheeks and she puts her head down so the boys cannot see her colouring. She was such a fool in front of her sons for even entertaining Frank. What must Petros and Spiros think of her!

'So is it not real then, Mama? Is there no flat?' Spiros needs confirmation. From that point of view, he is very like her, needs even what he knows spelled out in order to believe it.

'No, Spiros, there is no flat.' Her voice is breathy.

'Oh. So what do we do now?' His innocence is endearing. If they had managed to find a place for him to stay the next time she saw him, that naivety would have been gone. This country will strip it away as sure as the English get sunburnt when they go to Greece.

Chapter 34

They have missed breakfast and it is nearly lunchtime but Petros slips out of the room and returns with a tray loaded with a leftover breakfast buffet. Niki raises an eyebrow.

'I made friends with the girl who works in the kitchen,' he says as if this is the most natural explanation in the world. Spiros does not care. He dives straight in.

'You could have got her to make some fresh toast,' Spiros complains. Niki is about to reprimand him for his ingratitude when Spiros gives Petros a discrete nudge with his elbow and winks at his brother.

Even after they have eaten, no one has any energy. Spiros plays with the television until he finds channels for which they do not need to pay. They watch a film about a Pakistani man who left his country to try and find work abroad. Niki finds it all too close to parts of her life: the struggle, the loneliness, the displacement, but what impacts her most is how much the man from Pakistan is treated as if he has no value, as if he is a second class citizen just because his nationality is not that of the country he is in. It is not something she would ever have thought about in such direct terms but as she watches, she recognises the feelings that flash across the man's face and she looks at Spiros and then Petros to gauge their reactions. Their faces are blank.

They do not relate; this is just entertainment for them.

Is it inevitable, Niki ponders, that children become like their parents and re-act what they have witnessed, like she is doing, to some degree, bringing the boys here? Or does everybody act independently but only label the things they have witnessed before and notice those things that make them believe they are re-enacting the past? How much is wanting her sons to get an education in England influenced by her parents sending her to Greece to get a job?

'We watch our parents. The boys watch their babas and the girls their mamas and copy them,' Toula said. 'I watched my mama toiling away, getting up, lighting the fire, making the breakfast, cleaning the dishes and then cleaning the house. The hours she spent leaning over a tub washing our clothes, scrubbing away by hand. Then into the garden, tending the vegetables. The afternoon meal, another cooking epic, then tending to my baba when he came home. And he just flopped onto the day bed and did nothing as she continued working. More dishes to wash, his coffee to make, the sheep to take into the barn, the chicken to be locked up, on and on into the night after my baba was snoring and then up again the next day. Just the same as my Yiayia.' Toula paused to look at her mama's stiff portrait in the silver frame on the desk next to her grandchildren's smiling faces, bright and carefree.

'But at some point, if circumstances allow, things change. Our children are free from doing the things that we had to do. That is when they make independent choices. Until then, the choices that we make are all about getting our children to that point.'

She straightened the cushion beside her then, her twisted fingers tracing the embroidery that, presumably, her nimble fingers created when they were straight.

'That is why we are all so hypnotised, I think, by the Western world. They seem to be able to give their children choices with so little effort.' This comment was made just in passing, with no real weight.

Niki tried not to squirm in her seat. It was too close to the bone for her, reminded her of all she was trying to achieve for her boys, the size of the mountain she had set herself to climb.

'But I have strong belief in karma, my dear. Do you? I really believe that it is not the number of choices we have that makes the world a better place but the amount of kindness we show. It is certainly kindness that needs endorsing—rewarding, don't you think?'

'What are you thinking about, Mama?' Spiros asks. Petros is hunched over his phone and does not look up.

'Oh, nothing,' Niki replies and tries to remember what was happening in the film they were watching before she drifted.

'You were grinding you teeth,' Petros remarks.

'Was I?'

An exciting moment in the film takes the boys' attention again.

Spiros will do so well if she can get him here to study. He seems to gain real pleasure in learning, as if when a connection is made in his head, it goes past a pleasure centre, and makes him grin, giggle sometimes. It gives him real physical gratification. He will thrive and soar if he can stay here. As a result, his children will have all the choices in the world and will never live as she has lived.

Petros, on the other hand, seems to be in pain when he learns. It is real torture and every line is read with effort. For all that, he has still studied hard but he does it for the final outcome, not for the journey. If he can stay and study, it will not be the best time of his life but he will make it to the finishing line without a doubt.

Her lips tighten as the thought that he will marry well flicks through her mind's eye. That is not a route to encourage. If it happens, that's fine, but to aim for it is just not dignified. How many times had she been accused of that, with snide remarks and little innuendoes when she was younger, as if her love for Karolos was not real and would not last? Well, she showed them!

'Mama, you will hurt your teeth,' Spiros says.

Petros will do well all by himself and the beautiful girl he will marry will just be the icing.

Icing! Icing for him but not for her and Karolos.

'So far away,' Toula mourned so many times, in reference to her grandchildren.

Her own actions are leading to a lonely old age with grandchildren too far away to visit, just like Toula. Is that why Karolos has made such little effort to get them into university here? Unlike her, he has never even been out of his own country. It must be impossible for him to imagine visiting England. It's possible to imagine him staying at home and her visiting the boys in England on her own, just like Toula and Apostolis!

'*Panayia mou*.' She calls on her God at the thought of Karolos stuck in a lift for two weeks, suffering a slow death of dehydration in the summer's heat.

'Do you want to watch something else?' Spiros asks.

'No, no. I was daydreaming. It is not the film,' she reassures him.

'Come on, Mama. Look, I have brought *tavli*. We play a game, okay? That will stop you thinking about anything at all.'

The rest of the day passes in a hazy dream. Too tired to move and with little hope left, they do not mention the subject of the university. Petros manages to secure them some supper from his new friend in the kitchen and they go to bed early.

Niki has no idea what they will do. The still have tomorrow and the following day before her flight. Will they just sit around until it is time to make a last-minute scramble to get two more tickets for the same flight or does she book their return tickets now? But what if something happens so they can stay? She wishes she believed more in karma and that the world had a little more kindness.

Chapter 35

There was no point in them all traipsing round, so she sent the boys to the university for the day, to find out what the student's union is, to see the facilities first-hand. Perhaps they could locate the library, maybe even find fellow students on the same course. But their most important mission of all is to make friends with someone who would put them up for a couple of weeks until they find their feet. She feels sure that once they are actually at the university, there is bound to be someone willing to share a room or flat to reduce the payments. It's always a matter of who you know.

Meanwhile, she will go from one estate agent to another, one sign in a shop window to another, and try and read the local paper for rooms offered. She woke with a fire under her after being restored by a day of lounging and a good night's sleep.

Four hours later, having seen five estate agents and two properties that are each off the bus route and half an hour's walk from the university, Niki's feet are throbbing. She brought the wrong shoes. In her dream of giving her boys a better life, she wore her new pair.

Stepping off the curb to cross the road, she misses her step.

'*Gamoto!*' she swears without reserve as her ankle twists.

'Taxi, love? Oh, it's you. Small town eh? What's up?' Brian pulls alongside in his taxi and looks down into the gutter where Niki is staring at the heel of her shoe, next to an empty can of Strongbow. 'Oh, bad luck,' he commiserates with feeling.

'Anyone around for a pickup on Grove Road?' The radio crackles. 'Mike? Brian? Adrian, did yours show?'

'Where you going?' Brian asks Niki.

Pulling her eyes away from the heel, she surpasses the feeling that tells her she is beaten.

'Where is the cheapest place to buy shoes?' It is said as a joke, but Brian responds seriously.

'Ah, you could try Smithwicks. Hey, if you want to go there I can give you a lift if I take this pickup on Grove Road.' He presses a button on his radio. 'Got that, Ashley. Close by Grove Road; there in five.'

'Number twelve, Brian.'

'On it,' he says and presses the button again. The speakers crackle and the voices on the radio become muffled.

'You want a lift, then?' he asks Niki. Her smiles feel awkward. 'No, you're alright,' Brian laughs jovially. 'No charge. I'm on my way for a fare.' He leans over and pushes the door open. 'Hop in.' It sounds so cheerful.

'Is it far?' Niki has no sense of direction in this town. Everywhere looks the same. The ancient wall around the old town helps at times but on more than one occasion, she has mistaken one gateway for another and has walked twice as far as necessary.

'Put your seatbelt on please,' Brian mutters as an aside before answering her question. 'No, two minutes by car. How's your search going? Found the boys a place now?' His tone is so breezy, Niki would love to say yes and enjoy the lift in spirits. But she cannot lie.

'No.'

'Really? Is it really that hard?'

They drive on in silence. Niki blows air out through puffed cheeks. Maybe Brian has a spare room. There is no harm in asking. She has got to the point now where she has to try anything and everything.

'I don't suppose you have a spare room you want to let out, do you, Brian?'

He looks left and right as he pulls out into the next road. 'Ahhhh.' He draws the sound out. 'Doing a job like this has made me a man who likes his own space when he gets home.'

He didn't say he doesn't have a spare room.

'I mean for rent, Brian. You would get paid.'

'To be honest, a bit of peace and quiet is worth more than a week's rent.' He glances sideways at her as he pulls up to the traffic lights.

'What would make the possibility interesting for you then, Brian?' The words come out light, accompanied with a teasing look. What exactly is she prepared to do to get her boys here?

His sideways glance lingers for a moment this time. They pull away from the lights but then he immediately stops.

'I think this is where you get out,' he says.

The heat in her cheeks burns. Whatever had possessed her?

'No, no, pet. I didn't take you seriously. But this is where you get out. That's Smithwick's there, and I go right here.' He points.

Niki cannot meet his eye and she struggles with the door. Brian leans across her and opens it for her but when she tries to get out, she finds she still has the seat belt on and it locks rigid.

Brian releases it by depressing a button between the seats.

'I hope you find some shoes.' He's laughing now and waving as he pulls away. Niki summons all the muscles to make her mouth smile but she feels sure it must look more like a grimace. As soon as Brian has turned the corner, she looks down at the pavement, waiting for the heat in her cheeks to subside.

What on earth would the boys have thought if they had witnessed that? But then, it would never have happened if they had been there. She catches herself grinding her lower teeth against her incisors. She stops and feels the hole with her tongue. It has grown since she has been in England.

The inside of the shop goes on forever. It is bigger than any barn she has ever seen. It is the size of a football pitch, with banks of lighting that makes everywhere harshly bright.

The shoes are cheaper than even the weekly street market in Saros town. She picks the most modestly priced that she can find—thinned soled and rather ugly, and an acid yellow colour. Judging by the reduced price and the number of pairs on the shelf, they are having trouble selling them. She is not surprised.

The checkout girl does not know of any rooms to rent, nor does the security man at the door as she leaves. Sitting on the pavement by the door with a dog and a guitar, a man plays western tunes Niki vaguely recognises.

He must live somewhere, and he won't be charging a year's rent up front. She waits till the end of the tune.

The boys are waiting in the hotel room.

'Any luck?' Her first words come before she has even greeted them and asked them how they are.

'They have an indoor football field,' Petros enthuses.

'The library is enormous, Mama. Not just one room but five, shelves and shelves of books, but everyone is on the computers. There are many of them, lines and lines of them, a whole room, all connected to the Internet. You can use them for free when you are a student.' His eyes shine with wonder too, but there is also a sadness there.

'You can join clubs that take you to do things. Rock climbing, canoeing, sword fighting, only it had another name that I cannot remember.' Petros lies back on the double bed, his hands making a pillow, living in the world he has just seen inside his head.

'Fencing,' Spiros reminds him. 'And there are music clubs. It's possible to learn an instrument here. But I think the lessons cost. I'm not sure.' Spiros sits sideways on the chair, one arm over the back facing her.

'And the girls, Mama. I think they like the Greek men,' Petros chuckles.

Spiros gives him a derisive look before turning back to Niki.

'Mama, did you find anywhere?' Spiro's voice is quiet, as if he doesn't want to ask, or doesn't want to hear the answer.

She could tell them of the squat she visited, how she had seen a man smoking something called crack that made his eyes go funny as it blurred his consciousness. Would they even want to know that they could have a room there next to the skinny girl with dyed black hair and running mascara who talked constantly to someone who was not there? The guitar player himself was nice enough and most of the people in the illegal house seemed to be there only because they couldn't afford the cost of accommodation in the town. Generally they were friendly and enthusiastic about the idea of letting her boys stay, and she almost felt herself swaying. But when she asked about the boarded-up windows, she was told they had to remain so and that there was no electricity or running water, and the place ruled itself out in her mind. Then a man in a torn leather jacket with a tattoo of a tear under one eye said they were expecting a police raid, as they were 'cracking down on the real people,' as he put it. No. There is no point in telling the boys about that. It would be like offering a dog a bone but not letting it chew on it.

'No.' Her voice is quiet too and their eyes lock. Petros takes his hands from behind his head and lifts himself up onto his elbows to look at them both.

Chapter 36

They awake to glorious sunshine. Today is their last chance. Niki opens her eyes, expecting to feel either highly charged or completely defeated, but she feels neither. She feels dead, numb, exhausted, with not even enough energy to wallow in her failure. Lying on her back, the immaculate ceiling, with no cracks, no peeling paint, all new and appearing fresh reflects the quality of life she can see but is denied. Her boys fit here. They belong and yet at the same time it is not allowed to be. It is as if she has missed something obvious and if she could only see it, they would have places to stay and all would be well. But as long as it is not well, the feeling is one of not being good enough, a second-class human being who can only watch those at the party.

But these thoughts start to lose their energy and they drift away.

'Mama, are you awake?' Spiros asks.

'Yes, my sweet.'

'Mama, I'm tired,' he whispers as if to avoid waking Petros.

'Did you not sleep well?'

'I slept fine. I mean I'm tired of this, Mama, of chasing something that is not going to be.' Niki has to strain to hear him. 'It seems at every turn, there is a beautiful prize dangling, and then you turn again and they slap you for reaching for it. Then it appears again and it is just a little further away so you reach again, reach further, make a bigger effort, but you never quite get it. I don't like the feelings. I'm tired of reaching.'

Rushing out of her subconscious, a dream hurtles to the forefront of her mind.

'My daughter, she has grasped for the dream and reached it,' Toula said.

Was this a dream, or was it the conversation they had?

'The only part of her picture that was not complete was the mortgage. A heavy debt around her neck forcing her to make choices, stay in jobs that did not make her happy. Now that the sale of the clocks has paid that off, she has everything. Freedom. She wants no more except my company. It's a good feeling to know I could offer her that, now she can reach her real potential.'

The bird was back on her plate and she offered it the remaining corner of a sandwich.

'It made me wonder how many other people in my life were reaching but not grasping. That is the worst isn't it, reaching but not grasping? It has to be the most exhausting situation in the world.'

'Make a difference.' The bird had finished its crumb. 'Show kindness.' There was a key around its neck on a thin ribbon that dangled with no weight as it flew away.

'Mama, are you listening?' Spiros says.

'Oh, er, yes dear. I mean no, sorry, I was thinking of something.'

'I want to go home, Mama. They do not want us to study here.'

'I don't think there is any wanting or not wanting, Spiros. It's not that personal.' Sleep is gone. She is awake, his words gripping at her heart.

'We are the future. The next generation. We are who will dictate the next generation's old age and the way the world is governed. Of course it's personal,' Spiros hisses, still trying to be quiet but with his temper rising. He is wise, reflective for one so young.

'They do not see it that way, my love. I think, to a degree they want us. Three foreigners in a class are enough to pay the tutor's fee for the year.'

'So why do they make it so hard?' Spiros asks.

Is he crying? His voice has cracked. She looks across but his hair is over his eyes.

'I want to go home too, Mama.' Petros' deep bass voice sounds sleepy. 'It's too hard. Why bother?'

'It's too depressing,' Spiros adds.

All her drive and work and ambition melts in love and protection towards them.

'You really want to go home?' She must be sure before she can accept the relief of giving up.

'Yes.' Spiros is the first to answer.

'Yes,' Petros agrees.

'You want to defer to next year?' Niki asks. It would be such a waste to give up forever. They have learnt so much about how the system works and what they need. Next year, they will be so much more prepared. She will know how much money she will have to gather together. They will apply for rooms in the halls of residence at the right time now that both boys have got firm offers. Next year could be so simple.

'Okay,' Spiros says, but with no enthusiasm.

'Petros?' Niki asks, a tightening in her chest. Do they want to spend the rest of their lives as orange farmers?

'Of course,' he answers, but she cannot tell if he is just being diplomatic.

Heavy feet take them to the university. The bustle of the hallways is annoying, students get in her way, shout too loud, laugh too long, and generally act with excitement and carefree exuberance that she cannot share. The office where they can register a deferral is quiet. The woman behind the desk looks up, surprised by Niki's tentative knock.

They are there for a cold, impersonal ten minutes of bureaucracy and form filling and then they find their way to a travel agent, where the price of the return tickets, if they want to go all together on the same flight tomorrow, is at a height Niki could never imagine paying. To cut costs, they arrange for the boys take an earlier flight. She will see them on the plane and then wait a few hours in the airport for her flight. The boys will have to wait at the other end. The journey back to the hotel is completed in silence.

Chapter 37

The warm air of Greece is nothing like the watery sunshine of England. It is dry and silky and creates a heat haze over all they can see. Niki stands still to look, and breathe, the sun kissing at her skin.

As if the three of them have an unspoken agreement, they do not talk, they do not catch each other's eye. They travel silently all the way to Corinth and it is only with the knowledge that Karolos will be waiting there in the battered farm truck that prompts Niki to speak as the train pulls in.

'He has been alone whilst we have been there. He'll be all questions and energy,' she reminds her boys and herself.

But he is not all energy and questions. He greets the boys warmly but, for her, there is a reserve in his embrace. The boys say they are too tired to talk, but Karolos seems happy to be quiet. It is as if he has something that he wants to say, something of importance, but is holding back.

They all collapse once they are home, each on their bed. Niki tells herself that it is just for a brief snooze, but her fatigue is more demanding than she anticipated and she awakes to find it is dawn the following day. Reaching across her familiar bed, her fingers search for Karolos, but he is not there. Slipping on her thin dressing gown, she potters into the sitting room. The marble chip floor feels cool to her feet. Karolos is asleep on the day bed.

Through the shutters, the smells of the village—sheep, bread, warm earth and hints of cooking—allow peace to seep into her bones and the madness of the last week is highlighted by contrast and she wonders how the English manage living at such a pace all their lives.

With her cheek on the wood, she peers through the shutters to watch the village waking up. The *kafeneio* doors are open and a man leaning heavily on a stick goes up the three steps, right leg first on each level. At the top, he raises his stick in a general salute to all the other men who are already sitting, drinking coffee and smoking. A child is coming out of Marina's corner shop with a blue plastic bag that is too heavy for her, her free arm out to the side, balancing the weight. Thanasis the donkey breeder is leaning on the narrow shelf outside the window of the kiosk, mouth moving, deep in conversation with Vasso, who is unseen inside.

There is a brief smell of lighter fluid, which means Stella is next door lighting the grill. If she listens carefully, she can hear *rebetika* playing on the eatery's battered radio.

Nothing has changed. Everything continues.

'Are you making coffee?'

Niki jumps at Karolos' question. He stretches and yawns.

Without a word, she pads through to the kitchen. There are seven plates in the sink, seven forks, and three pans, one of which is badly burnt. After running water into this so it can soak, she fills the *briki* and adds the sugar, ready for the coffee. As it heats on the primus stove, she takes from the shelf a nearly empty packet of Greek coffee and makes a mental note to buy more.

Karolos is bound to start asking questions about England as soon as his coffee revives him.

He will want to know why she failed to get the boys a place to live when he saw so many flats available on the Internet. He will ask her questions about the way she dealt with things. Questions why she didn't do it the way he would have done it. Pointless interrogation to no end. All said very kindly no doubt, all very quietly, no direct accusation. She sighs.

She serves him his coffee and makes one for herself and sits down on the easy chair. Karolos puts his coffee down, makes a little cough, and opens his mouth. Here it comes, the barrage of fruitless enquiries about England.

'Constantinos called round,' he says.

Niki puts her coffee down quickly, palm to chest as she nearly chokes. Karolos leans forwards and pats her on the back. Her little fit subsides and she sits back, shaking her head as if the gasping and coughing was unexplainable, a simple random and unexpected occurrence.

'Constantinos?' she asks lightly. Her heartbeat is in her ear. Pinpricks of light dance before her eyes. Swirls of thought pass and repass the forefront of her mind. Images of her switching the computer off, covering her tracks on various transactions. No one can trace the money she took; the system is too disorganised. No, that is not the problem. Her heartbeat slows. The problem is Karolos will not be pleased about her having the job, especially one she has not told him about.

Her teeth grind.

He continues to sip his coffee, looking at her over the rim, but says no more.

'Oh, that Constantinos.' The laugh come out in a nervous spasm. 'What did he want?' She has put off the dentist because of the cost but the little hole behind her incisors needs attention. The sugar in her coffee is making her wince.

Karolos blows across the top of his cup to cool the brew, his gaze still unblinking. He still has not said anything more.

'I was going to tell you.' Niki knows she is offering too little too late. 'It started just a small part-time job, but the other girl quit and the boys needed the money for uni and...' She trails off. Karolos put his cup down but has not broken his gaze.

'We have a problem,' he says quietly.

'I was thinking of the boys. It seemed like the only way. In England, all the women work.' Niki stutters over the words.

'I do not mean I have a problem with you, I mean you and me have a problem out there.' He points to the front door, which is still closed. Once she is looking at it, she can hear the chickens' talon scratching to be fed. The gurgle of 'claww, uck' showing their impatience.

'Constantine has found out,' Karolos says, his voice still low but the words sound shouted, as if the whole village can hear. Niki hisses for him to be quiet as she glances to the boys' bedroom door. Her head swims. Ringing in both ears disorientates her. The hinges of her jaw ache as her teeth are clamped shut so hard, so tightly. Her swallowing reflex repeats itself with no control and her eyes become wet.

But her lips form no word. Her head shakes that it is not possible, the system is too chaotic, she covered her tracks.

'How?' is all she can say. So quietly it might only have been a thought.

'I don't think "How" is what we need to worry about,' Karolos sighs more than says. Her question seems to have confirmed to him that the accusation is true. A weight appears to push him into the day bed. A darkness shadows his eyes; his breath comes in shallow gasps as if he is pushing back emotions.

The word 'sorry' comes to the forefront in Niki's mind but it seems such a small word to offer and it will not alter anything. She can see what she has done through Karolos' eyes, through the world's eyes, and it does not look good.

Chapter 38

'I told him we would meet today,' Karolos says. Still, his voice is calm, no accusation, no anger, no sadness, nothing, just calm.

'Who? Constantinos?' The question sounds stupid to her own ears. Her fingers interlock, twisting together, and tears are squeezing from the outer corners of her eyes. She doesn't need an answer. 'For the boys.' It comes out as a whimper.

'And yet the boys are here.' His teeth are clenched now.

'When?' She can think of nothing better to say.

'Get dressed.' He stands, stretches briefly as if it is an unwanted inconvenience, then marches outside. The sound of a thousand kernels hitting compacted mud tells her he is feeding the chickens. In the bedroom, her suitcase sits unopened. It is too hot for any of the clothes she took with her anyway. She pulls out her normal work clothes from the wardrobe and then spots the red dress Stella gave her ages ago. Someone passed it to Stella but it was too big, so, as is the way with these things in the village, it got passed forward. Who knows who bought it originally?

The colour emboldens her.

It is not all red, but the large flowers printed on it are scarlet enough to have impact. The V neck is much lower than Niki ever wears but today, this is the dress. She has to hide behind something.

Karolos looks at her twice as she steps out into the sunshine. They get into the dirty truck without a word and drive towards Saros. When they are halfway, there Karolos speaks.

'We have one thing on our side.' He keeps his eyes fixed on the road through the dust-smeared windscreen. 'Constantinos is running in opposition to the mayor.'

Niki cannot see what this has to do with her taking money, so she stays quiet. She wants to ask if it is a small thing she has done, that would result in a fine, or is it something she can go to prison for?

Prison! What on earth was she thinking! Where would her boys be then? Her mouth drops open at her own stupidity. She didn't think. She had just seized the opportunity without regard for the consequences. The damned book! No wonder Apostolis threw it out! She crosses herself at his memory, three times, and then kisses her thumb, swearing under her breath at her own foolishness.

Karolos remains silent and parks the truck. In the harbour, the sea glistens as if it is just another normal day. As they walk towards the office, Niki takes Karolos' arm, but she can still think of nothing to say. What could be said to make what she has done right? Nothing! Maybe if she had come back alone, the boys at university, it would all feel worthwhile, but now! If she has to go to prison, who will get the boys to university next year? Not Karolos! He's been nothing and done nothing all his life. Useless! She lets go of his arm.

'Listen.' He stops walking. 'When we get in there, say nothing. Let me talk.' His eyes are dark. He is far away.

The air conditioned cool rushes out onto the street to meet them as they open the door, and Karolos takes the steps two at a time up to the office. There is a girl, chewing gum, sitting behind Niki's desk. She smiles an innocent greeting.

'I have come to see...' Karolos begins.

'Ah Karolos, Niki, er--' Constantinos turns to the girl. 'Go and get some more envelopes, please.'

'We have two unopened packets here.' The girl gets up and moves uncertainly towards the supplies cupboard.

'I want the long ones.' Constantinos takes a key from his pocket and unlocks the petty cash tin, hands her ten Euros, and writes the amount in a booklet that sits on top of the cash, locks it all up and replaces it. Niki's cheeks burn.

The girl leaves, fingernails tapping down the handrail, and Constantinos shows them into his office, where two wooden chairs are lined up in front of his desk. He invites them to sit down.

'So, it seems my trust was misplaced,' he opens.

Niki's fingers twist in her lap, her teeth grind into the hole at the back of her incisors. Karolos sits stiffly.

Constantinos throws Niki's notebook on the desk, the one she locked in her top drawer. It falls open to a page with a Post-it note stuck to it. On the Post-it note is written the address of the foreign woman who wanted a holiday let for her friends and family. On the opposite page is the list she began to make to keep her loans as just that: loans. The amounts she had taken and from whom are listed because, at the time, she fully intended to pay them back. But there are only four entries; the last one is incomplete.

'The first entry I could not check, because, as it was against the cash you took to the bank, there is no way of knowing. But I checked the second one against the records. We are not talking a great deal of money here, but I do not think that is the point.' Constantinos leans back in his leather office chair. The stem creaks with his weight and he talks directly at Karolos.

'So how much do those entries add up to?' Karolos asks.

Niki opens her mouth to say that there are many more than four, more like forty four. The amounts and people are tallied in the back of her diary, which she keeps in her bag. She lets the strap fall from her shoulder; her fingers busy themselves opening the catch. The diary's spine is face up. Karolos' big hand covers hers to stop her progress. Her fingers cannot move. He gives them a little squeeze. She closes the bag.

'Here, these, they add up to very little, but judging by the last entry, it is not a complete record,' Constantinos says.

'So you don't know how much in total?' Karolos asks. He puts his hand back to his knee and turns his body sideways, his arm loosely slung on the back of the chair. He shows no sign of concern and is talking almost as if he is discussing a business deal, which weed killers to use on his oranges, or maybe politics.

'The amount, at this stage, is unimportant. If we go through the records one by one, we will be able to trace back and see the difference,' Constantinos says gravely.

'And if you don't do that?' Karolos asks.

'What do you mean if I don't do that? It has to be done!' Constantinos pushes his weight forward. The chair creaks again and he rests his weight on his elbows and wrists on the desk. He is staring at Karolos.

'No, you misunderstand my question.' Karolos' voice remains calm and quiet. 'I am asking what would happen with your accounting system if you didn't use the man hours, which presumably you will have to pay for by the hour, to trace back through the, presumably, thousands of records?' There is a trace of a smile, inviting collusion.

Constantinos blinks, sits up straight, adjusts his shirt, the circle of sweat under his arms very pronounced. He blinks again and opens and closes his mouth.

'Nothing eh?' Karolos says very quietly, as if to himself.

There is a gap of silence which Karolos breaks with a jovial, 'Talking of man hours,' as if changing the subject. 'I have heard you have put in a fair few in your quest to oppose the mayor.'

Constantinos seems caught off guard by the change of subject and responds, obviously happy to be on easier ground.

'Ah yes, it is all networking, you know. Chatting to people, making friends.'

'Ah, not a game for me,' Karolos admits.

'No, it is not everyone's place,' Constantinos agrees. 'It takes a lot of work and time to make the right connections. Takes a man of strength of character I think, someone with vision.'

'Hmm, well, I am just an orange farmer, not a man of vision or of leadership,' Karolos says.

'Yes, leadership. That's the very quality needed to run for office. That and a good reputation.' Constantinos is smiling now, he eyes glazed over as if he is in a different place, remembering a different time.

'Ah yes, a good reputation.' Karolos nods and agrees but there is something in his voice that suggests there is more.

Constantinos searches Karolos' face to see if he is missing something.

'So whose reputation is on the line with regard to this water board office, Constantinos? You, eh?' Karolos pulls Niki's notebook towards him across the desk with one finger and then turns his head to read. 'Foreigners. Foreign names. What will happen when they find out that a few of them have been overcharged? And by how much? There is no way of knowing. And the others? The other foreigners, how will they know that they have not been overcharged? But who can say who has been overcharged and who is to say by how much? What happens if the Greeks think they have been overcharged?'

Constantinos swallows, this line of thinking obviously new to him.

'It could be a really big stink, could it not?' Karolos takes the notebook, closes it over the Post-it note and slips both into his pocket. 'It could ruin a man's chance if there were more to his life than just managing this office. In fact, could he really continue to manage the office when his bosses heard that such a thing had happened under his leadership?'

He stands. Niki follows his lead, her eyes fixed on him.

'It is a great shame Niki has to leave you so suddenly,' he tells Constantinos. 'But what with the boys staying at home now, not going to university this year, they will need their mama at home. You understand.' He holds out his hand to Constantinos to shake. There is a pause where nobody moves. 'And I really do thank you, on behalf of Niki, for your kindness in offering a month's pay in redundancy money.'

A frown takes a deep hold of Constantinos' eyebrows. He takes the proffered hand and as he shakes he pulls Karolos in towards him, kisses him on one cheek and growls, 'Don't push it,' and then he kisses him on the other cheek and almost pushes him away as he releases the handshake.

Karolos takes Niki by the waist and leads her down the stairs and out into the sunshine without looking back.

Chapter 39

Despite the absolute relief that overwhelms Niki, the drive back is just as silent as the journey into Saros earlier. Her relief started when Karolos first spoke up in front of Constantinos. The tightness that was constricting her breath, the band of lies and dishonesty that gripped like a weight around her chest, fell away. As Karolos spoke and took control of the situation, he grew before her eyes. The man she married sat there and the defeated farmer was nowhere to be seen. By the time he finished, he was her hero and her love for him bubbled in her heart. It continues to do so. She wants to stroke his face, kiss him, be held in his arms, but she can feel he is not in the same place as her. He is rigid, stiff-backed, unrelenting.

She wants to thank him but when she practices the words in her head, it sounds petty. It would feel good to praise him but she knows well enough that he will not want to hear praise. If she did utter any applause, he would tell her that he had done it to keep her from trouble, to keep the boys away from scandal, to keep his life calm and smooth.

She studies his profile, his skin so tanned from the sun and being outdoors all day every day. The proud orange farmer with the soft voice and the core of steel. 'Thank you,' she whispers but not loud enough for him to hear.

What would he really want to hear?

This thought sticks in her mind, dries her mouth. He has never been one to care for businesses or organisations or public face. In all of this, he will be thinking about the people she has taken money from, their suffering. That is where his concerns will be focused.

'I kept a record,' she says, the truck engine almost drowning out her words. 'I can work and pay them back.' Dreams of the boys attending university next year begin to swim, waver, melt away. Tears in her eyes spill down her cheeks. Karolos does not answer. He pulls in by their house and they go inside.

'Show me the record,' he says once the door is closed, his hand extended. Niki scrabbles in her bag, pulls out the diary, and opens it at the back page.

He studies and as he does so, a smile plays in the corner of his mouth which takes root and spreads to a grin and then a laugh, his head thrown back. Niki watches, wide-eyed. When his amusement subsides, he puts an arm around her shoulder and pulls her into him.

'Ah Niki *mou*.' He kisses the top of her head. 'Such an innocent.'

'What, why? You are not angry?'

'I thought you had stolen thousands. I thought I did not know who you were and that you had become a criminal mastermind.' He laughs again at this thought.

'No, look, here.' She takes the book from him and points out a three-digit amount.

'Ah yes, but that was from my thieving brother.' He laughs again. 'Niki mou, from the foreigners, you have taken almost nothing. Look, here you have taken two Euros and here three.'

'But it was wrong. I was wrong. I have seen England now. I have seen the place they must live their lives, the funny rules of their land. Their cities are so hard. I could not live there. They deserve every cent they get.'

'It looks hard to you because it is different. Maybe it is not so hard to them because it is what they know. It is their culture, what they have grown up with as being familiar, Niki *mou*.'

'So fast, though. No bending of the rules. Everything so rigid,' Niki says, her cheek against his chest, listening to his heartbeat.

'Yes, but the bending of the rules does not work so well, I think. Greece does not prosper as England does.' He rests his chin on top of her head.

The door to the boys' room opens and Petros staggers out, his hair sticking up, his track suit bottoms sagging on his hips. He yawns and sits down heavily at the kitchen table as if he is exhausted rather than someone who has just woken up from a long sleep.

'What's for breakfast, Mama?' he asks.

Niki takes out their sharpest knife from the drawer that sticks and begins to cut what is left of the bread. Petros goes through to the sitting area and puts on the television and becomes lost in a 1960s black and white Finos film. Karolos, sitting at the kitchen table, is deep in thought.

'Tell me,' he asks as Niki slices feta. 'Did Kyrios Tasso paying what he owed for last year's oranges have anything to do with your job at the water board?'

Niki feels her cheeks grow hot. It would be better not to say. No man wants to hear that his wife has stepped in and done his job for him.

'Niki?' he persists. She still does not speak. 'Okay, I can take by your silence it was. So what did you do?' He leans towards her and whispers with a quick look at Petros. 'Did you threaten to cut his water?'

'No! Well, not exactly. The truth is, I went to ask him for the money, that is all. He did the rest himself. He thought I was going to cut off his water, or charge him more or something, but I never said anything, I just asked him for what we were owed.'

'Ah ha.' Karolos sits back, deep in thought.

Spiros appears, yawning and stretching, grins at them both, slaps his baba on the back and sits at the table as if he is glad to be home.

They have feta and bread and eggs for breakfast. The chickens have been most obliging and the boys have two each.

Chapter 40

Niki and Karolos sit under the pines that top the hill overlooking the village. The pine needles coating the floor are soft and have trapped the heat. Niki's fingers dig in to reach for the cool layer underneath and she feels something move, an insect. She retracts her hand.

'Okay?' Karolos asks.

'Yes.' She looks down at the village, the burnt orange-tiled roofs a patchwork carpet sewn with a thread of whitewashed walls. Vasso is taking delivery of bottled water at the kiosk.

'Look, there are the boys.' Niki points. Petros and Spiros amble, hands in pockets, out from the back of their house and pass Stella's eatery. They approach the square and, seeing Vasso struggling with the weight of her shrink-wrapped delivery, they both jump into action, help her.

'They are good boys,' Karolos says. 'You have done a good job.'

Niki cannot answer. They are not in England. They are not being educated. How good a job has she done? She leans against Karolos to show her appreciation for his words. The boys, having finished helping Vasso, look a little lost as to what to do, turning first one way and then the other, finally settling on the bench that encircles the central palm tree. Thanasis the donkey breeder is on the *kafeneio* steps, hitching up his trousers before taking a cigarette from his top pocket. Niki can hear a murmur as he speaks, and the boys wander over to him. He puts a hand on Petros' shoulder and then the three of them stroll into the *kafeneio*. The boys take a seat by the window, the only dark heads amongst a sea of white and grey, and Theo comes over to take their order. Thanasis seems to be playing host.

'So that's it then,' Niki says.

'That's what?'

'All this fuss and effort, the boys struggling to get the grades they needed, the nightmare week we had in England, and now there they are, our boys, the new generation of orange farmers sitting in the *kafeneio* half the day.' Niki cannot hide the disappointment in her voice.

'We do not sit in the *kafeneio* half the day,' Karolos exclaims.

Niki doesn't respond. He has missed the point.

'Do you think we can send them to university next year?' She cannot see how they will be able to. They spent so much money in England with the flights and the hotel, the taxis and the food. Such a waste.

'Ah, that reminds me, I have something for you.' He shuffles to get to his back pocket but he takes on a look of first surprise and then recall as he pulls out a twisted parcel.

'Oh yes, and this came for you this morning.' He offers her the rather sad-looking package.

'Open that first and then I will give you my gift.' Karolos rests on his hand and then drops backwards so he is leaning on his elbows behind him, his legs stretched out in front. Somewhere in the village, a cockerel crows, a long raucous call with a quivering end.

Niki looks at the squashed parcel.

'What is it?'

'How would I know? The postmark says Athens.'

It feels padded, but it has a core of something rigid.

'If you open it, you will know what it is and who sent it,' Karolos teases her.

The package has been bound with sellotape and it proves hard to find the end or to tear it. Karolos takes a penknife out from down his boot. It cuts through easily but she takes care, as she does not know how much is padding and how much is contents. A letter is wrapped around the hard core, which has another layer of paper around it, and she tears this open.

'Oh?' Niki cannot make sense of it. It is a key, big and old and heavy.

'Odd. What's that for?' Karolos asks.

'I'm not sure,' Niki answers, but there is something familiar about the key. She flattens the letter on her knee and looks for the signature.

'It's from Toula.'

'I heard she has left, gone to England. I saw workmen in the house. Apparently the ground floor has been sold. They are making it into a taverna.'

Niki starts to read.

'Are you not going to read it out loud?' Karolos asks.

'Oh, yes, sorry.'

Dear Niki,
I hope this reaches you alright as I will be in England by the time you receive it.
We talked a lot, you and I, and we passed many relaxed hours over our coffees. You became like a daughter to me and I told you things I told no one else.

Niki stops reading and looks at Karolos.

'Karolos, I went to her house, when she was away.'

'Really? When? You mean the weeks when Apostolis was stuck in the lift?' Karolos cannot hide his surprise: a knot between his eyebrows there and gone in rapid succession repeatedly as he thinks.

'I was outside the door. Toula wanted me to clean, only Constantinos saw me and he asked me to work full-time. I actually had the key in the lock. This key.' She looks at it now with recognition. It seems like only yesterday and at the same time, a lifetime ago. 'I heard something, Karolos. I heard a call. It sounded like a cat.' She can almost hear it again now, but not quite. Was it more human or more cat? 'But I was so taken up with being asked to work full-time that the sound didn't really register. I heard and forgot, just like that.'

'Maybe it was a cat?'

'If I had not been so driven to grab every opportunity to get the boys to university, I could have saved him.'

'You don't know that.'

'Toula told me that what I heard had sounded like a cat. How did she know that unless she heard him, too?'

'What are you saying?' Karolos sits up, alert.

'I think she knew he was trapped and left anyway.' Niki loses focus on all that is around her. Would Toula do such a thing? But then, had she not walked away, too?

'Niki!' He sounds horrified.

'Well, she is not grieving, is she? She has just up and left for London as if her life with him amounted to nothing.'

'I think it is natural that she should want to be with her daughter. You must not say things that you do not know to be true, Niki. Read the letter. See what she says for herself.'

I told you things I never told anyone else.

Niki looks up. 'There, you see. I think she means about the noise sounding like a cat.'

'Read on.'

One of the things I told you was that I paid off my daughter's mortgage from the sale of the clocks. I have now another sum of money from the sale of the downstairs floor to the people in Saros who run the bakery. They want to make a taverna. This sale is going to give me a very comfortable lifestyle in London.

Niki stops to think about Toula in London, her little frame dressed in black, shuffling down a big city street. It is hard to imagine. But Toula with her grandchildren on her knees, enough money to spoil them, to give them the best education, that she can envisage.

'Go on,' Karolos encourages. He has found a thin twig and is using it as a toothpick.

Which leaves the apartment. The apartment! As lovely as it really is, it increasingly felt like my prison until you came to clean. You let in the light and laughter and tenderly polished it until it felt alive again. Without your company, I am not sure how I could have stood those last two years with Apostolis. I hope my eagerness to see you every time you came did not seem too strange.

Niki gasps. 'You see, she couldn't stand him.' She pushes the letter towards Karolos as if it is evidence.

'So? It does not mean she left him in the lift. Read on.'

'Oh my goodness!' Niki grips Karolos' arm as she stares at the letter. 'Listen to this:'

You see, there was one secret I did not tell you. I told no one, because that was his demand. Apostolis did not have long to live. He had a form of leukaemia. That was why he was so pale and thin. He refused to take any treatment. He became irascible this last year and feared everything might give him an infection. That was why the windows and shutters stayed closed, why he hardly ever went out. The longer I had to keep this secret, and the more fractious and inward thinking he became, the more I looked forward to your visits for some release. I hope that I did not become a burden to you?

Niki sniffs. Karolos abandons his twig and puts his arm around her. 'You alright, Niki *mou*?' he asks tenderly.

'Poor Toula! Why did she not tell me? I would have kept her secret.'

Karolos wipes Niki's tears away with his thumb. She takes a minute to compose herself and then, with a sniff, she reads on.

So as my daughter in London is now free to realise her potential and, as I have enough to keep myself in more comfort than I could ever imagine, I find that I am also in the very fortunate position where I can offer you the same thing. The key you hold you will have recognised by now. The papers from the lawyers will follow. If one day you are in a position to visit me in London, you will be so welcome. Meanwhile, do what you think best with the apartment. I wish you all the best.

Many many thanks and much love.

Toula.

Niki turns the paper over to see if there is any more, but the back is blank.

'I don't understand,' she says.

'Panayia mou.' Karolos hisses Jesus Mother's name. His eyes stretch wide as he stares at Niki.

'What? I don't get it,' she repeats.

'She just gave you her apartment. The upper two floors of that mansion on the seafront in Saros. *Panayia mou!'*

'No!' Niki stares into Karolos' eyes but she can think of nothing more to say. 'No!' She repeats herself.

'Yes!' Karolos fumbles in his back pocket and takes out a fat envelope that is rather worse for wear. 'That kind of belittles my gift,' he says, holding it towards her.

Niki takes it.

'I'm not sure I can take anything more in!' She cannot stop staring in Karolos' eyes, so beautiful, dark brown with gold flecks. So handsome.

'Why would Toula give me her house? Ah! She knows I know about her hearing Apostolis.' It is the only rational reason of which she can think.

'Nonsense, Niki. People don't have to be afraid to do kind things. She wants to give it to you for the years of happy company. You offered her life when her husband was offering death.'

'Maybe she knew he was going to die that week and didn't want to be there. Maybe she left him alone to commit suicide. She says he didn't accept any treatment.' Niki's mind races as she tries to make sense of it all.

'You can maybe all you like, but you will probably never know. Maybe dehydration was a better way to go than untreated leukaemia.' He shivers even though the sun is blazing. 'I, for one, do not wish to find out.'

'A house! On the seafront! In Saros!' Niki exclaims.

'What will you do with it? Will you sell it?' Karolos asks.

'You mean what will *we* do with it? I suggest we rent it out to tourists. A foreign woman who came into the office said there was a great need. Oh yes! That way I can pay back the money to the people I took from. You know, take it off the rent!' It all feels very unreal.

'Well, don't make too many plans yet. Let the paperwork come first. So you won't be needing this, then.' Karolos tries to take back the thick envelope which, although it is still clutched in her hand, she has forgotten about.

'What, oh, yes, what is it?' Niki opens it hastily, and euro notes fall out all over her skirt. A couple catch in the light breeze, which Karolos snatches back. 'What on earth?' Niki exclaims.

'Well, if you can do it, so can I,' Karolos says with a grin.

'What did you do? You didn't steal it, did you?' Niki grabs his arm with her free hand, the other still clutching the now-empty envelope. Karolos is laughing and scooping the Euros into her skirt so they cannot escape. She has not seen him look this carefree for years, not since the boys were small.

'No,' he laughs, 'I did not steal it. But if you can go to Tasso and let him get himself twisted in knots for last year's orange money, I thought I would give it a go to get the money from the year before that he owes us.'

'This is from Tasso?'

'Yup! Paid in full and,' he puts on his coy look, 'I also got him to pay what he owed Marina and he also promised to pay some old boy who apparently rings him daily saying he cannot even afford to pay his water bill because of him. So now he is straight with more or less everyone.'

'What on earth did you say? What did you threaten him with?' Niki starts to stack the money.

'Ah, well, I will be honest with you. I am rather enjoying the way you are looking at me. I feel a bit of a hero.'

'You are a hero! How did you do it?'

'Well, if I tell you that, maybe I won't be such a hero in your eyes anymore, so perhaps I might keep it a secret.'

'Oh come on. Tell me.' Niki gives him the envelope back, and he returns it to his pocket as she hugs onto his arm.

'Nope.' He is staring down at the village.

'Go on.'

'Nope.'

'You know what this all means, don't you?' Niki says. His arm goes around her and the two of them sit side by side looking down on the village, the plain, Saros in the distance by the bay that leads out to the rest of the world.

'This means the boys can go to university next year with no problem.'

Her gaze comes back from the sea of blue, across the orange groves, back to the village, and into the *kafeneio* where her boys are playing a game of *tavli*, a small cup of Greek coffee on either side of the board, Thanasis' chair pulled up to watch.

'Yes, but next year I suggest you ask them if they want to go.' Karolos is also watching the boys.

They sit in pleasant silence for a while. Niki's mind races to the apartment and the money. It is too much; it cannot be real. There will be a mistake. Or maybe not! Maybe this is her break, the break her parents envisaged, her freedom. A bird flies past, briefly blotting out the sun, light to dark to light. She lets go of her thoughts, accepting and letting her mind go blank. One minute they are up, the next down. The illusion of control over life is very seductive but in truth very unreal. Best to accept and seize the moment. In the distance, the sound of goat bells fades in and out with the breeze, dogs bark here and there, and a donkey at Thanasis' calls out its loneliness.

'You know, Niki *mou*. If you are really keen to set the boys up as well as we can, I have an idea.

Well, it is not exactly mine, but there is a way, especially now we have been so blessed.'

'A way?' Niki asks, looking up at him.

'Yes. There's this book I found...'

If you enjoyed The Stolen Book please share it with a friend, and check out the other books in the Greek Village Collection!

I'm always delighted to receive email from readers, and I welcome new friends on Facebook.

https://www.facebook.com/authorsaraalexi
saraalexi@me.com

Happy reading,

Sara Alexi

Printed in Great Britain
by Amazon